A Gangsta's Bitch 2

Leo Sullivan

A Gangsta's Bitch 2

Copyright © 2013 by Leo Sullivan

One

Monique lay on the ground in a heap, lungs on fire, depleted of oxygen as the formidable shadow towered over her. His breathing was labored like that of a pack-a-day smoker as he gasped for air. Hunched over her, he pulled back to swing the baseball bat, his face grimacing with malice, intent on doing serious bodily harm.

Suddenly, an ardent light shined across the parking lot.

A woman's voice screamed, "Bo, hurry!"

The voice belonged to Tatyana as she called out to her ac-complice. The other had already jumped back inside the truck.

Rasheed's car headlights illuminated Monique's body as she lay there. She screamed just as the car came to a halt. He couldn't believe what he was seeing. It was like a living night-mare; his woman being attacked by a white man.

Rasheed hopped out of the car and rushed over to her. The redneck swung the bat, causing it to whistle just inches from Rasheed's head as he ducked and rushed the big man. Rasheed swung wildly and connected with an overhand right that caught the redneck on the bridge of his nose, sending him spiraling backward. The baseball bat fell to the ground.

Bo threw one punch, nearly falling.

Rasheed was up on Bo as he rained blows down on his face and mid-section, opening up a deep gash on the white man's pale forehead, and another, as Rasheed drew back, striking with all his might. For some reason, the white man would not cover his face.

A truck sped up behind Rasheed in an attempt to run him over.

Monique screamed a warning.

Rasheed dived out of the way in the nick of time and rolled on the ground near the bumper of his car.

Punch drunk, Bo was barely able to stagger over to the truck to get in, his face a mess. The truck sped away, burning rubber, leaving behind a trail of smoke.

"Are you okay?" Rasheed asked Monique as he got off the ground, winded.

She saw blood on one of his knuckles. "My arm hurts, bad. I think it may be broken. When I fell, I hurt my ankle," she said, biting down on her bottom lip, making a feeble attempt to hold back her tears, as her body became racked with sobs.

He looked at his woman and it felt like a part of him was dying. It was unbearable to see her in so much pain.

She tried to sit up, but winced.

"Shit! Shit! Shit!" he cursed, enraged, as he balled up his fists.

He sat on the ground beside her. His heart was a river of emotions about to overflow its banks.

"Ba ... baby, I'ma hafta pick you up and carry you to the car so I can get you to the hospital," he said in the voice of a broken man. He was failing miserably at keeping the hurt out of his voice.

She rested her head on his shoulder and sighed deeply. In the distance a siren blared. In the sky, a lavender dawn was starting to peek over the starry horizon; morning's attempt to steal the night away.

"Oh Lord, Game!" Monique shouted as she suddenly re-membered she had come to her rescue once again. "Ra, you gotta go check on Game. She's hurt bad, please," Monique cried pungently as tears fell down her cheeks.

He frowned as he looked at her. "Baby, who you talkin' about?"

"Game, my friend. She's hurt real bad. You gotta help her."

Monique pointed with a trembling finger as she wailed.

Rasheed strained his eyes in an attempt to locate who she was talking about. Vaguely he could see a figure sprawled out on the pavement.

Monique tugged his shirt. "Rasheed, you gotta help her!" she pleaded.

He stood, eyes still focused on the spot in the distance. He took off running.

Game lay on the ground in a pool of her own blood, her body in a grotesque position, like a discarded baby doll that had been slung to the ground. Rasheed wasn't a doctor, but he knew instantly something was terribly wrong.

She looks familiar, he thought to himself. It then dawned on him – it was the flirtatious girl from the club. He swallowed the lump in his throat as he timidly crouched down to check on her. He could tell from the bubble of blood that rose from her nose that she was breathing. He rubbed at the back of her head to find the source of the pool of blood.

"Damnit man!"

She had a hole in the back of her head about the size of his fist. He pulled his hand away. It was covered in blood.

She was dying.

"I got to get her help. The girl is almost dead. It looks like her neck or somethin' is broken," he said to Monique as she sat on the concrete cradling her arm.

She grimaced in pain. "Mmm, my cell phone is dead, but Smitty the janitor should still be in the club," she said, panting, swaying back and forth in an attempt to find the fortitude to deal with the pain.

"I'll be back," Rasheed said. This time he headed for the club.

Moments later he was banging on the glass door. After Ra-sheed told the old janitor what happened to the girls, Smitty called the authorities.

Two

Rasheed & Monique

The police arrived in large numbers, enough so that they instantly made Rasheed nervous, the way they did lots of young black men. Monique sat in the passenger seat of Rasheed's car. Her arm was bruised black and purple. It had already started to swell.

The sirens blared a raucous symphony in her ears as a sea of police cars surrounded them in the parking lot. For a fleeting second she thought she saw fear in Rasheed's eyes.

"What happened here?" an authoritative voice asked.

He looked to be in his late fifties. He was of medium height with salt and pepper hair. His long nose was crooked as if it had been broken before. His blue eyes were hard to read, like a man who had been on the force a long time.

Monique did all the talking, but for some reason, the cop's eyes stayed on Rasheed. The atmosphere was quickly turning into pandemonium. The mighty roar of a police helicopter reverberated in the sky.

Rasheed couldn't help but notice that all the medical atten-tion was being focused on Game. Sure, the white girl needed it, but so did Monique. Off to his right Rasheed could see old man Smitty, the janitor, talking to a plain-clothes officers. The old man pointed in his direction as one of the officers jotted down something on a note pad.

"You say two white males and a female approached you in the parking lot, and it was over there that one of the white males struck you with the baseball bat?" the officer asked with one eyebrow arched.

"One of them picked her up," she pointed at Game, "and slammed her head on the ground," Monique said.

It was evident that she was in serious pain as she attempted to talk. At one point, it looked like she was about to pass out.

As Rasheed looked on, he was disturbed as once again like another day in the life of a Black man, he was confronted with one of his deepest fears, like some damn phobia—white men in blue suits. He pulled in a deep breath as what seemed like a thousand eyes bore through him with lingering suspicion.

The officer said, "Young lady, could you repeat that again?" His icy cold blue eyes continued to dart back and forth between them. It was all but evident that he was not buying her story.

Monique looked up at him with a wrinkled forehead as she held her arm.

Rasheed looked around helplessly.

On the other side of the parking lot, three ambulances sat parked as they attended to Georgia Mae. A few more moments passed and finally Rasheed's temper flared. Monique was in so much pain that tears cascaded down her cheeks as she retold her story for the third time. Rasheed could feel the blood rising in his face. The impulse to hit the officer in the mouth began to taunt him. Somehow it felt like he was being humiliated by watching Monique suffer and not being able to act.

Finally he had enough. With eyes blazing with fury, he spoke through his teeth, jaws clenched so tightly his chin seemed to jet forward.

"My fiancée needs medical attention and it seems like she's being interrogated instead of aided as a victim of a crime."

Rasheed's words caused the officer to jerk his neck back as he turned and looked at him. The officer was in his thirties with a chubby face and a hunched, rotund body.

"First off, you need to shut up and speak only when spoken to, and second, I need to see some identification."

"What the fuck does me having ID gotta do with her being assaulted?" Rasheed asked indignantly as he frowned.

It was then that he noticed that he and Monique were com-pletely surrounded as if the police expected them to make a run for it. They were victims of an assault, yet they were somehow being treated as suspects in a crime. All the smug faces and callous grins said more than a million words. A white woman had been assaulted and he and Monique were the next best things to an arrest.

In the distance, paramedics scrambled to get Georgia Mae into the waiting ambulance. She had a gauze wrapped around her head and one of the medics was holding an IV bag that dripped a clear liquid into her arm.

"Okay, buddy, let's see some ID," the cop asked again, waving his fingers at Rasheed.

Rasheed looked at him with narrow, slanted eyes as he shook his head in disbelief and fought with everything in his power not to lose his temper. He reached into his pocket for his ID.

The officer hollered to one of the other officers, "We're gonna need a female officer to search the girl here."

That was it. Rasheed exploded. "Y'all ain't puttin' a mutha-fuckin' hand on her. She needs medical attention. NOW! Fuck wrong wit y'all!!'""

"Calm down, these are normal procedures."

"Calm down?" Rasheed said, making a face. "Calm down for what, so you can continue to violate my fuckin' rights?"

One of the officers standing around commented eagerly, "You want me to place him in cuffs?"

Rasheed turned around to see where the voice had come from. It was then that he realized that the rest of the police were closing in. He prepared for the inevitable as he imagined the unfathomable, a white girl dying and he and Monique being accused of a crime they did not commit.

"Place your hands up, spread your legs," another officer said, walking up on him.

He had an attitude with Rasheed, and judging from the hate written on his face, he looked forward to seeing Rasheed attempt to resist arrest.

Rasheed retorted with a face of pure contempt.

"I didn't do shit. Put my hands up for what?" Rasheed chal-lenged.

Monique pleaded as she sat in the car sideways with her feet on the ground. She reached out to him, her voice cooed a warning.

"No, Ra, no." She winced in pain as the tears continued to streak her ebony cheeks.

But Rasheed's mind was gone to that place where a man's mind goes when he finds his back against a wall. If he allowed these evil men to handcuff him and place him in the back seat of a patrol car he would be considered guilty until proven innocent. For impoverished people that lived in the ghetto, that had always been the real law. Guilty 'til proven innocent.

"I said, put your hands up, turn around and spread your legs!" the officer said, raising his voice.

He was about five inches shorter than Rasheed and that made it all the better. It justified him using excessive force if need be, just like the Rodney King beating, only in this case, a white woman had been brutalized.

One of the plain-clothes detectives who had been talking to the janitor walked over, nudging his way into the crowd of officers that were about to pummel the tall, willowy kid.

"What's going on here?" he asked after making his way to within a few feet of them.

Rasheed spoke first, his eyes instantly recognizing that the detective in the suit must have ranked higher than the rest of the officers in uniform. "Sir, please help me," Rasheed said, his voice cracking as he swallowed the dry lump in his throat.

Rasheed continued as he cast a glance down at Monique. "My fiancée and her girlfriend work here at the club. They were attacked as they left work." Rasheed went on to tell him the entire story—start to finish—as the detective listened. What he couldn't tell was what he didn't know, that Tatyana was one of the assailants.

The way Monique was raised, she wouldn't tell on her unless it was absolutely necessary because, as crazy as it may sound, it was looked upon as snitching, and besides,

Tatyana hadn't gone to the police on her when Monique had whooped her ass.

After Rasheed finished talking, the detective looked around at the rest of the police standing nearby. His opaque green eyes were hard to read as he shook his head and walked over to Monique.

He crouched down, establishing eye contact with her, and said in a compassionate, fatherly voice as he gently touched her leg with the tips of his fingers, "Fire, are you alright?" He called her by her stage name. He had learned it from talking to the janitor.

"Nooo, my arm … I … I think it's broken." There was something about his caring voice that pulled a string inside of her, causing her emotions to spill over.

Rasheed turned away and stomped his foot on the pavement as he glared at the cop who had been so anxious to put the cuffs on him.

"I …" she said, trying to move her foot, "twisted my ankle when I was running," Monique sobbed.

The detective looked down at her badly swollen arm. He mumbled something under his breath and then pressed his thin lips so tightly together that they formed one line across his face. He looked at the poor kids; they were probably frightened to death. Gently, he patted her on her legs.

"I'm going to help you. How about we get you to the hospital, okay?" he spoke with kindness.

He stood back up, his cheeks flushed red as he twisted his face angrily. How could people that were supposed to help be responsible for so much hurt? There was no doubt in his mind what would have gone down had he not approached.

"Get a fucking ambulance over here. Now!" he barked.

Heads turned to look at him. "Why the fuck are y'all stand-ing around gawking? MOVE!" Just then his partner approached. With two fingers he held up a baseball bat, careful not to destroy any fingerprints that might be on it.

"Have this dusted for prints," the officer said as his eyes searched the ground for any more evidence.

Visibly shaken, Rasheed sighed in relief. As he leaned back against his car it felt like a large boulder had been taken off of his back. For the first time in his life, he looked at the police with real gratitude for coming to his aid.

"If you like, you can ride in the back of the ambulance with her," the detective offered.

Wearily, Rasheed raked his fingers through his hair and ex-haled, "Thanks."

Three

The Murder Scene

Lieutenant Anthony Brown bent down to examine the charred body of the victim. The horrible smell of burned flesh permeated the fog around the smoldering human remains. The doors to the Maybach limousine were open. Next to one of the doors was a discarded gym shoe.

For some reason, Lieutenant Brown stared at it, as if it could give some kind of hint as to what had happened.

"Lieutenant, there appears to be a bullet hole in the victim's right cheek, and judging by the markings on the ground along with the blood smear, it looks like the victim didn't die imme-diately. In fact, he may have tried to put up a struggle."

Mario Rodriguez was a Mexican detective with a reputation for busting cases. He had a thick mustache with bushy eyebrows and a tan complexion. He was in his late forties and worked out daily at the gym.

"Do you think he was shot after being doused with some-thing to make him burn like this?" Rodriguez asked as they both looked at the badly burned body.

The Lieutenant frowned as he cupped his hand under his chin. "This place looks death struck. There's a cold-blooded killer runnin' around this city. This wasn't just a murder; this was a message," Brown summarized.

A police officer walked by. Rodriguez made a face as he complained, "For Christ's sake, could you please walk around the other way? Don't they teach you guys how not to contami-nate a crime scene? Shee!" he exclaimed derisively.

"Sorry, pal," the officer said with a smirk, gesturing with his hands as he tiptoed away.

Lieutenant Brown touched the body with his latex-gloved hand and smelled his finger. "Gasoline?"

Two more officers walked by. Rodriguez shot them both mean glares. Brown stood looking at the crime scene. Dawn was starting to brighten the sky with an orange, Indian Summer glow. A piece of trash blew in the wind, and once again Lieutenant Brown looked down at the dead man's gym shoe as if, in some way, it could tell the tale of what happened to its owner.

Rodriguez said, "We got three victims, one fatally wounded. The paramedics say the chauffeur is going to make it. He was shot twice. He made a statement that a woman pulled a gun on him while he was outside of a radio station. He also said that a black male wearing a ski mask forced him in the trunk at gunpoint. The guy told him he'd better keep his mouth shut or else he was going to shoot him."

Lieutenant Brown walked over and looked at the bullet holes in the trunk and commented, "Guess he didn't keep his mouth shut."

Brown took a second look at the holes in the trunk of the car. He raised his brow and walked over to the bullet casings on the ground. The evidence technician had tagged and numbered each casing with orange markings, one through five. Lieutenant Brown removed a pencil from his breast pocket, reached down and picked up one of the casings with its tip. He examined it closely.

What he saw disturbed him greatly. He determined the cali-ber of the gun to be a nine-millimeter. However, the ammuni-tion was deadly, a Teflon-coated KTW metal-piercing bullet, better known as a "Cop Killer." For years the ammunition had been outlawed in New York ever since two armed bank robbers had held two entire police stations at bay, killing several officers and bystanders. The ammo was powerful enough to go through twelve telephone books with ease and still hit its target. Brown deposited the shell in an envelope and placed it in his pocket as he vaguely heard Rodriguez talking in the background.

"The other victim was shot in the ass," Rodriguez said.

"Did he tell you anything?" another officer asked.

"The only thing he could tell me was that the gunman wore a black mask. Other than that, he couldn't remember anything."

Rodriguez licked his thumb and flipped through pages on a small pad to make sure he hadn't missed anything.

"Someone had to drive the car while the gunman held the two victims captive," Lieutenant Brown reasoned as he ap-proached Rodriguez and the other officer. "And not just that, the kid, G-Solo, is not leveling with us."

"Why do you say that, Lieutenant?"

"He never mentioned the woman that the chauffeur spoke of. The first thing that runs through a person's mind when they're being abducted is, 'where are you taking me?' so his mind would have been on the driver. Remember, the dead man wore expensive jewelry and had over a grand in his pocket."

The two officers looked at Lieutenant Brown as if to say, "And?"

He continued, "G-Solo said he was robbed. Why didn't the robbers take anything from his bodyguard ... other than his life?" Brown asked on a somber note.

As he looked across the school parking lot, police vans, cars and various other police units scurried about like a small army. Bright yellow crime scene tape with black letters stretched the entire circumference of the lot. Brown paid close attention to the herds of media that had already begun to arrive. He looked up overhead where a news helicopter hovered.

"Lieutenant Brown," one of the techs called from inside the car.

Brown walked over and peered inside. The technician was a middle-aged man with thick glasses and a large balding head. He wore latex gloves which were visible as he pushed his glasses up on the bridge of his nose.

He pointed with his other gloved hand. "Here."

Brown squatted down. The inside of the limousine, on the right side, was stained with blood. Underneath the seats in the leg area, the tech had found two bullet holes and the casing to match. Brown bent down to examine the bullet holes. He reasoned that the victims had been shot inside the car as well. He briskly walked back over to the dead body. The pant legs were badly burned, but he could still make out the gunshot wounds to the victim's knees.

"Damn, you must have pissed somebody off bad," he said to the corpse as his mind churned.

Finally, the stench from the body overwhelmed him. He crinkled his nose and rose to his feet.

"Rodriguez!"

"Yes, sir," he answered from a distance.

"Get the DNA lab to analyze the car. Then have a profile run through the database to see if we get lucky and get a hit. Also, have the blood checked on all the evidence, especially everyone's clothing. Sometimes the killer injures himself." Brown bit down on his bottom lip as Rodriguez jotted down notes on a piece of paper.

Brown added, "Also, don't forget to get traces of hair and fibers. Find out who the limousine service belongs to and get their phone records. I wanna do a house-to-house check in this area. Somebody had to have seen or heard something."

"Why did someone shoot G-Solo in the ass, at close range, but kill his bodyguard?" Rodriguez asked as if talking to himself.

"He let G-Solo live for a reason," Brown confirmed. "I have a feeling this may be connected to the Damon Dice disappearance. It's just too close for comfort."

As he talked, something on the dead body caught his atten-tion. On the right side of Prophet's shirt was an outline of a bloodstain. It almost looked like a signature on a child's drawing. Brown took out his pencil and eased the dead man's shirt back out of the way to get a better look at the markings exposed in the charred flesh. Carved next to his nipple were skewed markings. Lieutenant Brown knotted his brow quizzically as he jotted down the letters on a piece of paper.

"Don't look now, but we got trouble comin' this way," Ro-driguez warned.

Brown's mind was elsewhere. Like all good cops, his instincts told him that the dead man had scribbled on his body with his fingernails; letters that could be just the lead he needed to break the case. A dead man talking.

"I need to speak to you," a curt voice said, causing Brown to look up. He eased the shirt back over the markings and stood to match glares with Captain Brooks.

"Damn, why don't you just try putting in an application for a job at 75? It'll save you time and trouble from making the trip all the way out here," Brown said without humor as he placed a hand inside his pocket.

"Good news travels fast," Brooks said, looking down at the body on the ground with a satisfied smirk on his lips. "Especially if it's one of your good men at the 75 who tips me off."

Brown ignored the last remark. "So what gives you reason to barge in on my territory this time?" Brown asked, barely able to contain his disdain for the man.

Just then, the medical examiner arrived. Both men turned to watch Dr. Wong. He was a very small man, about five feet tall with shoes on. He wore spectacles as thick as pop bottles. In the strange world of police work, Dr. Wong was considered a multi-genius. He held several different degrees. He was also a lawyer, amongst other things. Momentarily, both men stopped talking and nodded their heads toward the doctor, acknowledging him.

"Morning, gentlemen," the doctor said, bowing his head slightly.

He and Lieutenant Brown were close, having even sat in the morgue on a few occasions and drank beer as they talked about the gory details of a case.

The doctor placed a pair of latex gloves over his child-sized hands and squatted down, going right to work. To some in his profession, Dr. Wong was an odd man. Some would even consider him a little off his rocker, but all agreed that when it came to the science of crime scene investigation, he was a genius.

As he reached down to examine the body, he frowned and spoke to it as if he expected an answer back. "A bullet entered your right cheek. I can't be sure until I get you on autopsy table, but it look like the temporal, occipital, parietal and frontal bones of your skull have been shattered." Wong made a face and peered closer at the body.

"Jesus, what he shoot you with, an elephant gun?" The doc-tor's eyebrows stretched upward.

"This homicide may be connected to the disappearance of Damon Dice," Captain Brooks was saying to the lieutenant. Their volley of words were heated, nearing a shouting match. Brooks continued, "If that's the case my department needs to be abreast at all times of the goings-on of this case, no matter how small they may be."

Brown looked the Captain in the eyes and stated bluntly, "Didn't you just tell me earlier that you had a spy in my depart-ment in the 75?" Brooks arched his brow at the lieutenant as Brown finished his statement. "Then I think it would be in your best interest to use him, because until my superiors tell me so, I ain't tellin' you shit about this case."

As the two officers argued, Dr. Wong continued to meticu-lously go over the body, talking to it as if it were a dear old friend.

He discovered more gunshot wounds as he pulled back the deceased's shirt. The doctor looked up to get Lieutenant Brown's attention and Brown just so happened to look over at Wong. He silenced him with a warning look. The last thing he wanted was for Brooks to know the dead man had left a clue as to who the murderer was.

"I take it you haven't seen this morning's paper?" Brooks shouted with his finger in the young lieutenant's face. "The media, along with certain people in high places, including myself," the angry Brooks got up in Brown's face causing him to take a step back, "believe the disappearance of Damon Dice is connected to the East Coast, West Coast beef. The same beef that took down them criminals Tupac and Biggie Smalls. You know, a rivalry."

Brown made a face as he shook his head. "Listen man, this ain't got jackshit to do with a fuckin' rivalry. You and I both know it. There's a madman on the loose running round this city, and I got a feeling that until we find him, there are going to be a lot more killings," Brown said, fuming over the Captain's ignorance.

The two men continued to argue. Everyone around them stopped what they were doing to watch. Lieutenant Brown, the younger of the two, didn't intend to back down. Dr. Wong looked on as the Captain made the crucial mistake of jabbing Brown in the chest with his index finger, not once, but twice, causing Brown to look at the finger and frown, as if it were a deadly disease.

Brooks lifted his finger a third time to jab Brown in the chest, but before he could, Brown drew back and knocked the older man out cold.

"Oh shit," Dr. Wong said as he looked on.

That was the day Lieutenant Anthony Brown made one of the biggest mistakes of his life.

Four

Jack and Gina

Gina Thomas lay awake in the darkness listening to the old house settle as it cracked and shifted, making noises as gusts of wind could be heard throughout, like ghosts rumbling through it.

She pulled the thick quilted blanket up to her chin. So much was going through her young mind. Jack had called her a bitch the other night while they were pulling off the lick with G-Solo. It wasn't just that, he had gone on a tirade about her being dumb for buying the watch in her real name. She admitted to herself that it wasn't the brightest move. She remembered him saying that he was going to stop by the jewelry store in the morning, personally, and retrieve the information from the Arab jeweler. She knew what that meant. Murder. But not if she could beat him to it.

She reasoned that all she had to do was get the information out the cabinet where she remembered seeing him file it. She didn't want Jack to take the risk of going into the store. He was moving too fast, taking too many chances. Now this.

Jack stirred in his sleep, lassoing his arm around her. The security of his arms felt so good. Like him, she had waited a long time.

She felt his hot breath on the nape of her neck as his large hands began to roam the contours of her body. He eased up her Victoria's Secret nightie. She wasn't wearing any panties. She lay still, faking sleep. Just about every night it was the same thing. Since he had gotten out of prison, Jack was like a sex fiend. At one point she even had to buy some K-Y Jelly for lubrication. He was beating in her guts so much she stayed sore.

His hands palmed her ass. She could hear his breathing, feel his breath on her back. Then she felt his dick on her butt cheek, probing. He asked in a husky voice dripping with lust, "Boo, you 'sleep?"

She didn't answer, not yet. He eased closer. He kneaded her breasts. She felt his dick crawl between her thighs as she lay on her side. She turned over and faced him in the dark.

They both felt the cold draft at the same time. She had acci-dentally pulled the covers off their feet. Jack pulled the covers back down. Her hand came to rest on his muscular chest, more so as a divider, a quiet request for him to desist.

She needed to talk, but Jack needed sex. That was the one thing she had never denied him, her sex or "his pussy" as he liked to call it. He had trained her, taught her so much, even showing her how to use the muscles in her pussy to contract and tighten so that she would know how to milk him, please him. She wondered if he was going to ask her to give him head. Of course, she knew she would comply. Gina knew the secrets to keeping her man. What she wouldn't do in bed, another woman would.

"Jack, we need to talk," she said, feeling his dick jabbing her in the stomach.

"Talk?" he repeated as he squeezed her breast so hard that she almost screamed.

Instead, she sucked in a deep breath as she felt her nipples grow hard at his touch.

"You called me a bitch the other day."

Silence.

Finally, Jack spoke, "Ma, that was my head speaking, not my heart. Things was movin' fast. I was frustrated. I needed to bust them niggas' ass, you know, make a statement."

"Jack, it hurts when a nigga refer to his lady as a bitch, I mean " she said suddenly. "Yeah, I know, I'm that ride or die bitch, your gangsta bitch, a bitch that know how to rock a nigga to sleep, but it hurts in a way that I can't explain when a nigga call his shorty a bitch and it's said with malice," she said in a small voice.

Jack's hand sailed across her nipple as two fingers gently caressed her breast. He inched closer, his mind considering the right words.

"I know you wanna take over DieHard Records and put the whole industry on smash, but in the process you gotta respect me. And in the end, I'ma let you do you," she said as Jack walked his fingers down her breasts toward her stomach.

He ran his hand across her pubic hairs as he inched a little closer. "I'ma play my position," Gina said, talking in the darkness, her voice slightly muffled by the thick quilted blanket.

Quiet awkwardly consumed them. With Jack, Gina could be sure when she had overstepped her boundaries for pillow talking.

She changed the subject, "You hungry? You want me to go downstairs to fix something to eat?"

"Naw."

"You want me to roll you a blunt?"

"Naw, I'm good," Jack said, taking his hand off of her and turning onto his back.

Gina could sense that Jack's mind was now elsewhere as she bit down on her lip. She tried to read his thoughts, but came up blank. Like most women who are determined to do anything to keep their man, she wondered if she had said the wrong thing or perhaps hadn't said enough.

She reached down and grabbed his dick. He was semi-hard.

She stroked him to life. She could feel him grow in her hands veins thick as her fingers. She squeezed his dick and it pumped back like it had a mind of its own, responding to her hand manipulation.

Jack released a deep sigh of pent-up energy as she placed her thigh over his legs. He reached down and palmed her butt cheeks, spreading them so wide that two of his fingers nestled comfortably in her pussy.

They were on their sides, face to face, and she responded to his touch by licking his chin like he was ice cream. She nibbled on his lip, grinding her torso against him as her tongue drove down his neck. Hot saliva mingled with the moisture that was starting to form on his body. She licked his hairy chest like he was something sweet.

As he moved his two fingers expertly within her, she moaned against his flesh. The room was no longer cold, they were on fire as the covers fell away from her backside. Slurping sounds escalated as moans serenaded the darkness. Even though she was still sore, she dared to want more of his sex.

Boldly she started talking like a teasing lover.

"Jack," she said, her voice a breathless whisper against his skin. "I want you to fuck me … fuck me hard." She said it like a command as she humped his hand.

His fingers stroked her clitoris, stirring her passion. She was so wet and slippery inside, the sensation almost drove her crazy.

"You think … you think I don't appreciate you … us," Jack said with his words slurred like he was drunk off of lust.

Gina had a way of doing that to him. She had a way of doing that to any man. Not even he was immune to the wiles of her feminine enticement. But tonight he was going to entirely flip the script on her.

His fingers were dripping with her juices like honey.

"Now, how 'bout I serve you?" he asked, taking her com-pletely by surprise. He reached over and pulled her on top of him. His nature was so hard that it felt like a steel pole against her stomach as the warmth of their bodies smothered his dick.

She raised her body slightly as she licked his chest, beckon-ing him. Gina's thighs were almost as thick as his; her ass bounced as he heaved her upward. He was interrupting her rhythm until she realized what he was doing.

"I want you to sit on my face," Jack said, not waiting for her answer.

Gina giggled.

Jack imagined seeing her face in the dark as he positioned each one of her thick thighs on the side of his face while she sat her ass on his chest. He buried his tongue in her as his fingers spread her lips. He lapped and licked as her pubic hairs tickled his nose. He found the little man in the boat and just sucked and tongue-lashed it until Gina started to grind on his face.

"Oh, shiiit, that's it. Yeah, yeah that's it. Hmm, suck it! Suck it!" He spread her lips wider, burying his tongue as deep as it would go. "Oh, my … oh, shit … shit. I'm gonna cum in your mouth." Jack grabbed her butt, making her pussy press tightly against his mouth. With his teeth, he gently bit, licked and lapped at her clitoris and used his entire face to rub across her sex while he took his tongue on a trip down south in a circular motion and dipped it in and out.

Gina threw her neck back as he massaged her labia, his mouth dripping with her juices. He returned to her clitoris, mounting an assault of pure ecstasy. He sucked on her greedily, non-stop, until finally she exploded with his mouth still locked tight on her pussy. She released a stream of cum that flowed in what felt like an ocean. Her orgasm rocked her body in spasms. He continued to suck as his tongue molested her like it was taking more than she could give, thrashing, exploring. "Oh, Jack, that's enough, that's enough! I … I …I can't take it … any … more," she intoned, throwing her head back like she had whiplash.

Jack held her in position with his arms tightly holding her thighs in place, pussy center to his face. He worked her G-spot until she screamed. It was like some kind of gravitational pull. His hot mouth sucking on her clit. How could something that felt so good drive her insane?

"Oh, Jack, I'm cumming again!" she exclaimed as her eyes rolled back.

She rode his motions as they ebbed and flowed, her body trembling and shaking. He never ceased or slowed. If anything he went faster ... faster. Deftly, his hands spread her skin and his tongue found another spot, a wall.

God, where did he learn that from? she thought in the back of her mind as she pleaded out loud to deaf ears. "Oooh wee, you're torturing meee, yesss!" A tear spilled from her eyes. One more orgasm like that and she would be climbing the wall.

With all her might she threw her body back, and she pulled away. Like some gigantic suction cup, she was released. Her supple breasts were covered in sweat. Her hair was matted to her face and she sucked air like she had just run a hundred yard dash.

Gently she grabbed his dick, placing it into her mouth. In-stantly, she tasted his sweet pre-cum, savoring the taste on her tongue. She tried to deep throat him, but gagged, he was too big, so hard. She deep throated him again, up and down ... up and down. Her arm felt numb from the uncomfortable position she had landed in when she threw herself off his body.

She turned around with him still lying on his back and straddled him in a sixty-nine position. She continued to take him into her mouth while her hands played with his balls, saliva dripping over her fingers. He dug into her sex. Leaning up he bit down on her butt. The sensation only seemed to excite her more. She worked him with the same determination to bring him to ecstasy as he had her.

With her hands she waxed his penis up and down with the juices from her mouth as she sucked hard. She traced his dick with her tongue as he moaned and grabbed her

head, placing his dick back into her mouth, a silent signal to
her that he was about to cum. She wanted him down in her
throat, but Jack enjoyed cumming on her chest, massaging
his load all over her large breasts.

She found her rhythm as her pace quickened. "That's it.
Suck that dick. Uh ... watch your teeth."

He moaned with his hand on her head, forcing her to
go deeper—and she did. Gina wasn't the best at giving
head, but she got points for swallowing.

Suddenly, she stopped as she turned around to face
him. She heard him take a deep breath and curse in the
dark.

"Gina, what did you stop for?" he asked vexed as he
groped for her in the dark. He felt her take hold of him as
she shifted her position.

"Please baby, cum inside of me." Her mellow voice
quivered with a hint of a plea.

He swallowed hard, determined to bridle his sex. He
could feel her move next to him on her back. She had never
taken her hand off his rigid hardness. Slowly, he rolled onto
her, spreading her legs wide with her thighs wedged against
his.

He placed one of her legs on his shoulder. Gina gasped
in anticipation of what was coming next. With dick in hand
she could feel him prodding, searching her pubic hairs.

With her legs wide open, the scent of her sex was in the
air. He eased inside of her hot spot as his mouth greedily
came down slobbering on her breast as if he really thought
he could force her whole titty in his mouth. Inch by inch,
he was sliding right in. She was so hot and wet that his first
deep stroke, flesh against flesh, sounded like a French kiss.

He went deeper with her legs spread wider. She squirmed and wiggled as her claws dug into his hairy, muscular chest. She tried to scoot up, but there was nowhere to go.

"You wanted me to fuck you hard," he stated as he eased inside of her a little deeper.

She bit down on her lip and threw her head back on the pil-low as she arched her spine to meet him with a thrust of her own. He followed her invitation and drove his dick in as far as he could. Gina stifled a scream as she grunted and groaned with each one of his powerful thrusts. She clung to him as if he were a black stallion she was losing control of. He was so deep in her body that he was hitting a spot that felt like a nerve.

"Oh Jack, oh Jack. Ba ... baby gooo slooo," she pleaded.

His pace was so fevered that it felt like someone was pounding a battering ram inside of her. Then it happened, his body turned into a human volcano. Saliva trickled from his mouth onto her breasts as he shivered and shook, back arched. He pulled out of her and cum squirted like a faucet all over her stomach, chest and face, enough to lotion her body with. Satiated, depleted, he plopped down on her body, winded, gasping for breath.

Sleepy-eyed, Jack rolled over onto his back as Gina reached down for the thick quilted blanket. She could feel the goose-bumps on her arms. The room had suddenly taken on a chill, as she shuddered, teeth chattering. She needed to go to the bathroom.

Instead, she snuggled into Jack's waiting arms, careful to avoid the cold wet spot in the bed, evidence of their lovemaking. She could feel his heart beating with a rhythm of its own, powerful and strong. His skin was moist and warm, soothing against her body.

This was where she needed to be, wanted to be, in his arms, forever. She sighed tranquilly, like a woman who had just achieved multiple orgasms. She closed her eyes and was about to doze off.

Jack said groggily, "Wake me up in the morning. I'ma go holla at dude at the jewelry store. I don't like movin' like this." Jack's breathing was heavy as sleep toyed with his brain. "You know where the stash is, just in case..." he said.

Gina's eyes stretched wide open as she was brought back to the reality of her blunder – leaving her real name with the jeweler. She knew what he was talking about, just in case. In other words, he meant in the event he did not make it back.

Gina lay perfectly still listening to the noises in the old house. For some reason, she felt the urge to cry. Everything was going so right. Lord knew they had taken so many chances and somehow managed to get away. With a million dollars stashed away, not including the jewelry they had taken, how could everything that was going so right, suddenly go so wrong? There was no way in hell she was going to let Jack take the chance of maybe walking into an ambush if the police happened to follow up on the lead at the jewelry store.

Sunlight was starting to stream through the window as she stealthily eased out of bed while listening to Jack's light snoring.

The old wooden floor creaked under her bare feet as she crept over to the dresser. She picked up Jack's gun as he stirred in his sleep. Her heart pounded in her chest as she stood as still as a mannequin. There was only so much that any man could take. Jack was a thug. She knew that he was going to beat her ass when he woke and found she was gone with one of his guns. If she made it back home with the application, she reasoned, Jack would be relieved. She used the bathroom, took a quick shower and left for a place of no return.

Five

As Gina drove, she felt like she was racing against time. There was no way of knowing if the Arab who owned the jewelry store had already contacted the authorities, anxious to get the reward money. She knew she was taking a great risk, but it was better she than Jack, she reasoned.

She parked her car downtown, almost a block away from the jewelry store. With the pistol safely in her purse, she exhaled as she looked in the mirror and donned a pair of sunglasses. She adjusted the blond wig on her head. Her hand trembled as she puckeredher lips to apply lipstick. She had a bad feeling she couldn't shake.

Her intuition was telling her that something was going to go terribly wrong. She ignored it, took a deep breath and exited the car.

Showtime.

An elderly white man with a shopping bag brushed against her. She paid him no mind as she continued to walk briskly, looking straight ahead. Her eyes narrowed as she searched for anything unusual. She studied the jewelry store across the street. She could feel her chest tightening as she watched pedestrians traverse the streets. She could smell the sweet aroma of food coming from somewhere. It was 8:31 in the morning.

Suppose he has someone in the store with him? she thought.

As she neared, she realized that the security gate of the store was not opened yet. Her pace slowed, and for the first time, she thought about turning back.

A young man with freshly braided hair, so neat that it looked like it had been painted on, bumped into her, hard. He was talking on one of the smallest cellular phones she had ever seen.

"Damn. Yo, watch where you goin'!" he huffed, frowning.

Then his eyes softened as he took her in. His gaze fell to her wide hips.

He suddenly smiled as he watched Gina abruptly turn and walk away. She walked over to the newsstand, pretending to be interested in a magazine, something to do with Weight Watchers. She held the magazine in her hand and looked at the others on the stand. There was a picture of Oprah with big hair on her magazine, "O," and at the bottom of the magazine rack was a newspaper with a picture of Damon Dice's face splashed across the front page. Gina's heart did somersaults in her chest as she read the headline:

"Music Executive Damon Dice still missing, presumed dead. Case may be connected to the East Coast, West Coast rivalry …"

Just as Gina was about to reach for the newspaper, she saw the proprietor of the jewelry store arrive. With his briefcase in one hand, he opened the gate with the other while his shifty eyes looked around. Like most foreigners, the Arab was very conscious of his surroundings.

Gina took off in a trot, her heart racing in her chest as her mind signaled a warning. She crossed the busy street with her hand in her purse and her mind paying no heed to the silent warning. As she neared and her pace slowed, her mind quick-ened with each step.

The Arab, with his back to her, opened the gate and took one final look behind him, but didn't seem to notice the pretty girl watching as he entered the vestibule of the store. He had inserted the key into the door and was about to turn off the silent alarm when Gina walked up. Her shadow fell across him.

Startled, he turned around and faced the black woman who had an icy cold demeanor. She wore dark shades and her lips slightly curved up to the right. The Arab noticed the gun poised in her hand, aimed at his chest.

"Do as I say, and you won't be harmed," Gina spoke calmly.

"Okay, okay," the frightened man said with his eyes bulging as he looked down at the gun.

He raised his hands in the air.

"Put your hands down and open the door," Gina ordered as she waved the gun at him. The Arab complied. In doing so he triggered the silent alarm. Gina walked inside, remembering where she saw the man file her paperwork.

At that very moment, police were already headed for the jewelry store.

Gina made the man lie down on the floor. A tuft of straight dark hair fell over his forehead as he took his time getting to the floor. He continued to hold onto the briefcase as if his life depended on it. He watched Gina with what looked like mischief on his tanned face. His thick beard, bushy eyebrows and piercing black eyes made Gina feel something was not right about his character.

She had only come for the application with her name on it and was going to be out of there in a dash, but there was something about the way he held onto the briefcase as he lay on the floor. It wasn't fear she saw in his eyes, it was something else.

"Gimme that briefcase, Muslim!" she said, raising her voice, gesturing with a wave of the gun.

"No!" he said as he continued to shake his head adamantly and clutch the briefcase to his side.

Gina leaned down and pressed the nine-millimeter to the back of his head.

"Let it go!" she yelled.

He complied as he mumbled something under his breath about Allah. Gina opened the briefcase. To her disappointment, all she found was an assortment of papers, a palm pilot and a thin calculator. The damn Arab was watching her intensely.

Just when she was about to close it, something told her to look inside one of the small side pockets. She did and found three black velvet pouches. Bingo! Diamonds, large and uncut. She quickly stuffed them into her pocket. In the back of her mind a voice was warning her.

On the floor, the Arab squirmed around as he began to curse in his own language. At one point, Gina was almost sure he was going to get up and try her. Time was moving fast, but the voice in her head told her she was moving slow, way too slow. Her inexperience would cost her as she turned away and headed for the filing cabinet.

The phone rang, startling her. As fast as she could, she scanned through the " T" section in the filing cabinet, found her application, careful not to leave any fingerprints, and shoved it into her pocket. As she turned around, the store owner pointed a gun at her and fired. The impact of the bullet knocked her backward. She staggered into the file cabinet. His next shot missed.

She crouched down and fired with her eyes closed. She was acting purely on instinct and fear. She managed to get off a fusillade of shots, hitting the store owner in the upper chest and neck.

He keeled over backward, his gun, a small caliber .22, slid across the floor. Gina took off hobbling. She could feel warm blood soaking her pant leg and running into the heel of her shoe. She grimaced in pain as she headed for the door with her gun concealed under her jacket.

Outside the police were arriving as tires screeched to a halt directly in front of her. She felt trapped as she held her jacket together at the collar. Underneath, with the other hand, she held onto the gun.

"In there! In there!" she screamed, pointing frantically like a woman terrified as she turned and back-pedaled.

She had the best disguise in the world. Who would ever sus-pect a beautiful woman to be a cold-blooded killer? At least that was what she was relying on as she blended in with the rest of the people in the early morning on their way to work.

Lieutenant Brown got out of his Caprice. His trained eyes scanned the crowd as he entered the store. He quickly notice a trail of blood coming from out the pawn shop.

Immediately, his radio crackled to life, "There's a gunshot victim in here, a possible homicide. Secure the area!"

He ran to the door with his eyes following the blood drip-plets and saw a woman with blond hair in the near distance who was hobbling badly, like she was hurt, trying to get away.

"HEY … YOU!" Lieutenant Brown called out to the wom-an.

The woman took off in a trot. No one paid any attention to either the Lieutenant or Gina, as if they were in a world all their own.

Gina tried her best to blend in with the morning commuters on their way to work as she weaved in and out of the crowd.

Gina tossed a look over her shoulder, praying that Lieute-nant Brown would not recognize her. She turned a corner. Her hip hurt something awful. She was almost at her car … just a few yards more.

"Hey, you, stop!" Brown ordered.

She turned around, surprised that the cop had gained on her. She thought she had lost him. He was too close. The crowd of people stood around her like a human barrier, protecting her from his capture, but still he was closing in fast. She needed to act quickly.

With no other recourse, Gina came up firing two swift shots. Instantly, pandemonium erupted as people screamed and scurried in all directions, stumbling all over each other. Lieute-nant Brown crouched down and aimed at Gina's back as she ran away.

"Too many people. Fuck!" he cursed and continued after her.

This time he ran after her with caution, haunted by the glimpse of her face.

Up ahead, at a busy intersection, the light had turned red. A middle-aged white man wearing a cowboy hat and leisurely smoking a cigar drummed his fingers on the door of his SUV. Gina approached him and flung open the door.

"Get out the car, cracka!" she hollered, with her wig on sideways.

"Huh?" he jerked his head around, looking at her dumb-founded as she pulled on his shirt collar.

He resisted by holding onto the steering wheel for dear life as he bit down on his cigar.

Gina looked over her shoulder. "Damnit!" The cop was ap-proaching fast. She fired two shots into the driver's face, causing chunks of flesh to fly in the air. She pulled him from the vehicle, throwing him to the pavement, and hopped in the SUV as a staccato of shots rang out, hitting the steel and fiberglass.

Gina ducked down, punching the gas pedal. The vehicle leapt forward as the tires screeched and the car fishtailed. She ran the red light and barely avoided hitting a yellow school bus. She sideswiped an oncoming car. Gina sped away in a daring getaway in broad day light in downtown Brooklyn. All she left behind was a trail of burnt rubber, empty bullet shells and dead bodies.

Lieutenant Brown ran up and raised his gun to fire at the departing vehicle, hesitating as he looked down at the lifeless body of the man who had been snatched from his vehicle. He made a futile attempt to check for a heartbeat.

The entire left side of the victim's face was missing. Brain matter and skull fragments were on the pavement. The revolting sight forced him to turn his head as all around him people scurried about in panic, on the precipice of madness.

An ambulance's shrill siren blared in the distance as patrol cars arrived. Lieutenant Brown happened to look at the ground next to the body and for the first time he noticed the bullet shell casing.

Carefully he reached down to pick it up. His breath lodged in his throat. The ammo the woman was using was KTW. Brown had a gut feeling the bullet would match the ones they found at the homicide of G-Solo's bodyguard, Prophet.

"Did you get a good description of the shooter?" a voice asked, causing Brown to look up into the bright morning sun. The brief image of Gina flashed in his mind. He recognized her from somewhere, but where?

As sweat gleamed off his forehead, he responded, "African American woman, light-skinned, blond hair—"

"Woman?" the officer retorted, surprised.

Brown shot him a glare for interrupting. "She appeared to be wounded and to have lost a lot of blood. I spotted her leaving the scene at Hasan's spot."

A voice cut in. It was Detective Rodriguez.

"We found a body back at the jewelry store. The owner was gunned down. There's lots of blood. From the looks of it, it was a botched robbery attempt, but I can't be for sure. There's a surveillance camera in there, so I'm gonna have the tape taken down to the station to see what we can find." As an after-thought, Rodriquez added, "Hasan was determined not give up his property."

"Yeah, and it cost him his life trying to be a hero," Brown said on a more somber note.

At least they had video of the robbery. Maybe that would be just the big break they needed. He hoped.

A few miles away, police helicopters raced over the horizon through the dense clouds and thick New York smog. It spotted the red SUV and instantly lowered, careful not to touch any electrical wires in the small enclosure between the buildings.

"You, the occupant of the vehicle, get out with your hands up, walk ten yards and lie flat on the ground spread eagle!" the police ordered.

Dust and debris stirred on the ground in small tornados as the powerful rotors lowered, descending on the vehicle.

Half a block away, Gina limped, dragging her leg as her eyes desperately searched for a place to hide. She used the side of a building for support. She continued to walk as best she could. Up ahead she saw a Laundromat. She was beginning to black out as she held onto the wall.

A police car sped past her. An old black woman folding clothes looked up at Gina, whose pants were soiled with what looked like blood.

She frowned. "Lord have mercy."

The old woman's hands never stopped moving as she watched the young black girl limp inside the Laundromat. Their eyes met, young and old. The older woman's five-year-old granddaughter sat in a chair, legs swinging.

She played with a black Barbie doll. The little girl watched Gina struggle to walk.

"Ma'am … I'm hurt … bad. Could you please help … me?" Gina said as she held onto the edge of the folding table, blood caked under her acrylic fingernails.

As Gina spoke, police cars zoomed up and down the streets. Overhead the roar of a helicopter could be heard.

"Oh my God, child. What have you done to yourself?" the old woman asked with tears in her eyes.

Her voice cracked as she shook her head. Strands of unruly gray hair sprouted from her loose ponytail. Her skin was a deep, Hershey chocolate brown. She had deep age lines that formed creases and made her once beautiful face sag like a woman who was always sad, even when she smiled, which wasn't often.

"Ma'am, I'm in a lotta of trouble," Gina winced, looking over her shoulder as she spoke to the old black woman.

The old woman looked at Gina with concern as she walked over to the door and looked out. The police had completely surrounded the block. She turned the orange sign on the door, "CLOSED." She then turned around to see Gina on her cellular phone.

"Jack! I'm hurt … bad baby … you gonna hafta come get me.

I'm at the Laundromat on 27th and Main," her voice qui-vered.

"Fuck! Gina, I told …" Jack was shouting into the phone, but realized it wouldn't do any good.

He quickly got dressed. He put on his bullet proof vest for the occasion and grabbed his .380 and was out the door. He drove his Benz to the area he knew all too well, it wasn't too far from where he was.

Six

Jack Lemon

Jack drove while surveying the neighborhood. The spot was hot and the place was crawling with cops. The police had the block sealed off and weren't letting any traffic in or out as they did a door-to-door search with dogs.

"Shit!" Jack cursed as he drove with the burner on his lap.

Up ahead, he saw the Laundromat. The sign in the window said it was closed. He prayed Gina was safely in there.

What the hell did she do? he wondered.

A helicopter hovered overhead. It looked like some shit straight out of the movies as throngs of police, some of them wearing riot gear, marched down the street.

"Ginaaa!" Jack droned as he pounded his fist on the steering wheel. "How am I gonna get her outta this?" he questioned himself.

As Jack turned the corner, his mind raced against the clock in his head. Then he had an idea. It was risky as hell, but he had to try it. It wouldn't be long before the police made it to the Laundromat.

Jack drove around back about a block away and parked his car, leaving it idle. He got out with the .380 concealed in his pocket. He cut through an alley that led to a gangway which led to another.

From his position in the narrow gangway he could see all the passing police cars. With gun in hand, he hunched down, obscured in the shadows. He waited as a police cruiser passed. Jack raised the gun, aimed and fired three shots at the police car. He took off running back through the alley. By the time he made it back to his car he was walking casually as he watched police cars abandon their search and rush to the scene where the police car had been fired upon.

The police car that had taken the shots called in for help. "Officer down! Officer down!" was the cry on the police radio.

As Jack cruised back toward the Laundromat, he noticed a SWAT team van and a host of other police vehicles race by him, all headed in the direction of the infamous call for help.

Jack parked in front of the Laundromat and quickly got out. His eyes scanned up and down the street. As he walked up he noticed that someone had thrown a bleach solution on the ground. He pounded on the door. The old woman who opened the door wouldn't look him in the eyes. A little girl sat in a chair cradling a brown baby doll as she softly cried. Gina lay on the floor in a puddle of blood. Jack felt something in his chest tighten as he looked down at her unconscious body.

"Ah, fuck, Gina! Nooo!" Jack's voice choked up with emo-tions as he ambled over. His heart ached in his chest at seeing Gina this way.

Taking a deep breath, he felt his eyes grow misty. The old woman and the child looked on. The little girl was crying in sobs that racked her little body. Jack made a face, that of a pain-stricken man. For some reason, the old woman would not look him directly in his eyes.

Jack snatched a blanket off the folding table and began to carefully wrap Gina's body in it. She moaned softly, fluttered her eyes momentarily as he picked her up. Already, the blanket was soaked in her blood, him too.

He picked her up and headed for the door. The old woman raced ahead of him, opening the door. Still, they exchanged no words. He nodded his head; she wiped a tear, a simple gesture that conveyed so much. As he walked out the door he prayed like hell that they would go unnoticed. It was only a few yards to his car, but it seemed like miles.

Gently he placed Gina in the back seat and got into the front. He steered the car in the opposite direction of the police and headed for a destination where he was sure someone would look after Gina – Rasheed's grandmother. She used to help all of the wounded Panthers back in the day. Some say she even helped Assata Shakur after her daring escape from a maximum security prison after being unjustly convicted and sentenced to life, for the murder of a State Trooper.

Chapter seven

Rasheed & Monique

The police had finally taken Monique to the hospital
and they allowed Rasheed to ride along in the ambulance
with her. After her wounds were treated, she was
questioned at length, by two plain-clothes detectives. Her
head spun. Monique wanted to scream at them because she
felt like in some ways they were still viewing her and
Rasheed with suspicion.

Now, as if in some kind of fugue, Monique stared down
at the hospital's linoleum floor like she didn't know how
she had gotten there. An elderly man with a walking cane
sat across from her, sleeping with his mouth wide open.
Monique was fortunate, neither her arm nor her ankle were
broken, just badly sprained. The doctor told her she would
heal within a week or two, but what about Georgia Mae?
Would she make it?

Rasheed placed his arm around her. She sniffled and
dropped a tear as she scrolled her eyes up at him. In a small
voice, she asked, "What made you come to the club? You
showed up—"

"Monique Cheeks?" A husky, but polite, voice
interrupted her question to Rasheed, causing her to tilt her
head in the direction of the emergency room door just as a
woman was pushing a small child by in a wheelchair.

Monique raised her hand, wincing in pain at the
motion, and the doctor walked over. He had an

assortment of fancy pens in the breast pocket of his white jacket. His eyes, with bags underneath, looked tired. Patches of gray hair ringed his head. He talked with caring gestures, very animated with his hands and neck. For reasons unknown to her, Monique, with her lips pressed tightly together, stared at the pens in his pocket.

After the doctor had introduced himself, he went on to ex-plain that her friend Georgia Mae Hargrove had a concussion, a hairline fracture to her skull that required fifteen stitches, and a bruised spinal column.

The doctor arched his brow as he stated frankly, "Georgia Mae is a marvelous specimen of a female, her physique, her sinew. If she wouldn't have been in the shape she was in, she more than likely would have died from her injuries, or would have been paralyzed for life."

With the doctor's statement, Monique's hand flew to her mouth in shock.

As if having a second thought, the doctor scratched his chin and looked at Monique. "Are you a dancer, too, young lady?"

"Not no mo'," Monique retorted.

The doctor slightly nodded his head in agreement.

"Can we see her?" Monique asked as a woman walked by silently weeping.

The doctor glanced at the woman with a genuine show of concern, and then looked back at Monique. For a fleeting second, she thought he was going to tell her no.

Finally he answered, "Yes, please follow me."

He led them to Georgia Mae. As he walked away, his coattail drifted behind him. Awkwardly, Rasheed stood behind Monique while she struggled with her crutches to walk toward the emergency room door.

Silently, Monique sat in a chair next to the bed. Georgia Mae lay still, almost serene, under the crisp white sheets, arms folded, one over the other. The white bandage on her head was stained red. For some reason, Monique could not get out of her mind, no matter how tight she closed her eyes, how Game looked like she was lying dead in a casket.

Monique noticed the bruises and lacerations on her face.

"Shit," Monique cursed under her breath.

She came to my rescue again, and now she's lying there like she's in a coma, she thought.

Once again, tears rimmed in Monique's eyes. Suddenly Georgia Mae stirred underneath the covers. A hand with a broken fingernail moved just a little, but enough to give Moni-que a signal.

"Game?" Monique called her name.

Georgia Mae's eyes fluttered open like butterflies.

Monique scooted her chair closer. Georgia Mae turned and looked at Monique. A warm smile tugged at her lips.

"God, I thought you were dead," Monique said, taking a deep breath and rolling her eyes up at the ceiling.

"Child, pah-leze. ATL bitches don't get kilt, we gets crunk," Georgia Mae said in her best ghetto, countrified, but strained voice. She attempted to laugh, but instead she frowned. "Damn, my head hurts." Her eyes darted away from Monique to the figure who was standing away from the bed.

Game smiled for the

first time. She then looked at Monique. "Yo, what he doing here?"

Monique looked at Rasheed and asked, "Do you two know each other?"

Slyly, Rasheed shot the white girl a warning glare.

"No, we don't know each other. Do we?" Rasheed said, continuing to warn her with his eyes.

Game just stared at him and made a face. Pain. Her pink tongue primed her thin lips as she swallowed hard like her tongue was made of sandpaper.

"Naw, I don't know you, dude." She turned her attention back to Monique. "Girl, are you alright?" she questioned as her hands drifted to her head, feeling the bandage.

"Just a few bumps and bruises," Monique replied.

"I can't believe I did some dumb shit like that. I could have taken both them rednecks out easy," Georgia Mae said balling her fist up. "I kicked that cracka square in the face. Thought he was out for the count, but that fucker got me from behind."

"It wasn't your fault," Monique said placing her hand on Georgia Mae's arm.

"Yes, it was. My instructor always taught us, when you get a man down, punish him." She shook her head and continued to

touch the bandages. "I thought they were old. They were just old junkies with young bodies. And Tatyana, I got something for that long neck bitch."

"Yep, me too. I gotta admit, ole girl had intentions of killin' me," Monique said and then asked, "did you tell the police that she had something to do with this?"

"Hell naw," Game shot back. "She didn't tell on you when you got that ass at the club."

"Y'all mean to tell me y'all know who did this?" Rasheed questioned.

Monique and Georgia Mae exchanged glances with each other, agreeing to keep his ass out of it. Rasheed was about to say something when his cell phone vibrated on his hip. He turned away to answer it and began speaking in hushed tones.

"The doctor says they're gonna have to run a few tests on me, hold me for a week or two," Game lowered her voice and pursed her bottom lip. "At first I couldn't feel nothing in my legs, now they're both numb with a slight tingling sensation." She had the kind of fortitude that let you know she was a strong-willed woman.

"You have any family here in New York?" Monique asked, her voice filled with sympathy.

Game shrugged her shoulders and made a face like she was taking a stroll down memory lane.

"Naw, I don't have any family here."

"Who's going to take care of you once you get out of the hospital?"

"Ah, girl, I'm going to be okay. I've been taking care of my-self ever since I went off to college," Georgia Mae answered.

"Nah," Monique sighed, "you're comin' to stay with me."

Game stretched her lips to the side of her face and rolled her eyes. "Girl, I couldn't impose on y'all like that."

Rasheed walked back over to the bed. His face looked like all the life had been drained out of it.

"Gina been shot," he said with a slack jaw, mouth agape like a man in shock.

"Oh my God!" Monique muttered as she exchanged looks with Rasheed. "What the hell is goin' on? Is she okay?"

Rasheed just nodded his head with a distant look in his eyes.

Moments later, they rushed out of the hospital and caught a cab to his Grandmother's house. Jack greeted them at the door. He looked terrible. The two old friends hugged each other. Monique hugged Jack, too. Rasheed had never seen Jack look so distraught in his entire life.

Jack raised his brow when he noticed Monique with the crutches and her arm in a sling. They sat on the couch and gave each other details of what had happened, each story more devastating than the other. Jack had relied on the fact that Grandma Hattie was a nurse who would always help people, black or white, if they needed medical attention. There was no way in hell Jack could have taken Gina to the hospital. By now they were all crawling with cops looking for a woman with a gunshot wound. The bullet had entered her thigh and come out. She had lost a lot of blood – too much – but Grandma Hattie said she would make it.

She would take care of Gina for the next few weeks. She said being a nurse was a true gift from God, doing his will, healing the sick.

Eight

Two Weeks Later

Lieutenant Brown

Like someone piecing together a mysterious puzzle, Lieute-nant Brown had started to fit all the pieces together from the murders that his department had infamously named the "Death Struck" cases, due to the particularly hideous nature of the deaths. He had been working on the cases around the clock for the past forty-eight hours.

Finally, the first big break came. The security camera in the jewelry store where the Arab was robbed and killed had actually captured footage of the shootout and murder. However, when they went to view the video, to Brown's dismay, it was of such low quality that it was hard to discern the actual features of the person. One thing was for sure, the killer was a woman and she moved with confidence.

Brown drank black coffee from a Styrofoam cup and re-wound the video over and over, as images of the phantom woman moved across the screen. Even after she was shot, she moved with a swagger as she removed some papers from the filing cabinet. There was something about her gait that disturbed Brown as he strained his bloodshot eyes at the snowy picture on the TV screen. After staying up all night in his office going over the video, about the only thing he was sure of was that the black woman wore a blond wig.

In his mind he could still see her firing shots at him as he chased her. It was something in her eyes and not just that, the wig. The blond wig. Blond … wig.

Brown's mind churned as he took a sip of his coffee. Sud-denly it dawned on him. Did the mother of Damon Dice say that a young woman wearing a blond wig came to pick up the money as her dying son had requested? He frantically waited for the ballistic report to come back to see if the bullets from the jewelr y store murders matched those of the brutal murder of G-Solo's bodyguard, Big Prophet. The bullets still weighed heavily on his mind.

Brown had a hunch. It was a long shot, but he figured he had nothing to lose. He got on the phone and had one of his men retrieve the records of the cab companies in the Coney Island area. There were a million cabs in the naked city. It was a job that could take months or longer, but if they found the cab driver, maybe he could identify the woman who picked up the money … and maybe even locate the killer's location.

There was a knock at his office door. Detective Rodriguez opened it slightly and stuck his head in. His shiny hair was slicked back on his head, still wet from his morning shower. Sleep's shadow was cast on his face as he munched on a large glazed donut.

"We got a match on the jewelry store homicides," Rodriguez said in between bites of the donut.

"Yes! Yes!" Brown chanted and swung his fist in the air.

Rodriguez then added, "The Chief wants to see you in his office ASAP."

A Gangsta's Bitch 2

As soon as he walked in, he knew that something was terri-bly wrong. He could tell by the long expression. Chief Daniel Steel, with his hound dog eyes and receding hairline, was a no-nonsense man.

"Have a seat," he said to Brown as he took off his spectacles.

Brown sat down. As always, the picture on the cluttered desk caught his attention. It was of a little girl about ten years old. She was holding a soccer ball and standing in front of a yellow school bus. Her teeth were severely crooked, just like the Chief 's.

Chief Steel exhaled deeply as he shuffled some papers around on his desk. "I'm going to get straight to the point. You're being taken off of the Death Struck case and suspended indefinitely."

"Whaaat!?" Brown screeched, bolting straight forward in his seat.

The Chief silenced him with a glare and continued, "You struck a superior officer. If you had reported the matter to me, maybe I could have had it taken care of. However, it was reported to Internal Affairs downtown."

"That's bullshit!" Brown yelled, standing up, nearly toppling the chair over. "That man put his hands on me. I have a right to defend myself."

"No, you should have reported the matter to me. Promptly."

Brown frowned with disgust for his boss. "Chief, the man was trying to belittle me in front of my men and the entire 75th . Where I come from you don't put your hands on another man. Period!"

"Yeah, and where I come from you don't strike another of-ficer, especially the likes of your kind."

"My kind? What the fuck is that s'posta mean?" Brown asked, enraged, taking a step closer, lips pressed tightly across his teeth.

The two men stared at each other. Brown couldn't believe what he was hearing. Not only was it some racist bullshit, but he was being suspended and removed from a case that he felt he was close to cracking.

"I just can't believe you'd take me off the case after all the hours I've put into it. It's bad enough that I'm being suspended, but what's the reason for removing me?"

Silence.

Brown went ahead and tried his last card. "Chief, I found a match between bullets found in the jewelry store murders and the ones found at the murder scene of the rapper's bodyguard. The connection may be a female. I'm having records of cab companies checked and a composite of the woman made. It's the same black woman, blond wig."

The Chief 's eyebrow rose as he placed his elbows on the desk. He was obviously impressed with the progress Brown had made on the case. He looked at the younger man sternly. "You're a good cop, but you crossed the line and you have no one to blame for this but yourself. I want you to go clean out your desk," the Chief said as he reared back in his chair as if that were the end of their conversation.

Brown was filled with a stirring desire. He felt that it in-volved something bigger than what the Chief was telling him. Disgusted, Brown simply gathered his thoughts and walked out the door. As soon as Brown was gone, Chief Steel picked up the phone and called a friend. Fate may have finally shone favorably on him. He couldn't wait to deliver the information he had just learned from Brown. Certain people in high places were always looking for a little free publicity. Everything he had just learned, he relayed to his friend, assuring him that Brown had been taken off the case.

Now it was just a matter of time.

Scrambling to check with the cab companies, the Chief ran a ballistics check himself. Now that he had learned that it was a woman in both cases, he would send the video of the jewelry store murder to Washington, D.C. where the best crime scene technicians in the world would have the picture of the woman enhanced and quickly identified. The payoff in the end would be great, just as his friend Captain Bill Brooks had promised him. Brooks would get the glory in front of the media for cracking one of them thug rapper murder cases and he would get a bonus, along with his retirement from the Mayor's Office. That was an offer he couldn't refuse.

Nine

Jack

Jack pulled up into the Marcus Garvey Projects driving Gi-na's sleek black Jeep Cherokee with tinted windows, sitting on 22s. He sipped on an Olde English 800, while a blunt smoldered between his fingers. On his lap was a new chrome-plated nine. He placed the pistol in his waistband and turned up the bottle to take another long swig. He belched like a frog, wiping his mouth with the back of his hand.

As he got out of the Jeep, he left behind a trail of Chronic smoke. Jack waved to a few heads in the parking lot who he knew. A chick wearing blue jeans and a white halter top called his name. Instantly he recognized her from back in the day – big booty Pam.

She was now a smoker. Some said she was on that shit, and by the frantic way that she waved at him, her large double D's threatening to expose themselves from the confines of her halter, Pam was definitely on something. If it wasn't crack then it damn sure was dope boys.

It was Saturday night, and a brilliant full moon hung in the majestic sky like a waxed coin embellished with scattered stars. Jack had a nice buzz from good weed and drink, but not enough to make him lose his focus as he walked. In the back of his mind, he couldn't help thinking shit was lookin' lovely. As he liked to say, shit was bubbling. He hadn't been out the joint a minute and his grind had come up big time.

He thought back to Gina and how she took a bullet. At first he was pissed at her for doing some dumb shit, but when she gave him the diamonds, well, a nigga had to give her props. Like no other chick he had ever known, Gina kept it gangsta to the utmost. The stones she stole were probably worth close to a million dollars.

As Jack walked, bopping through the Marcus Garvey Projects, he felt like a big ole pimp stacking paper, pulling capers, plotting on not just the rap industry, but the entire game.

Jack knocked on a door while carefully checking his sur-roundings, still conscious of where he was. He watched every-thing in his peripheral vision. Nina, his nine, was snug in his drawers. Just as he looked over his shoulder, the door opened. An attractive white girl was standing in the doorway. Jack did a double take at her then turned to look at the number on the door.

"428," he muttered and scratched his head, craning his neck to look at the next door. He knew the weed he had just smoked was good, but damn. "Ah, mmm. Yo, I got the wrong address," he mumbled with his eyebrows knotted together in confusion.

The girl giggled. "You looking for Rasheed and Monique?" she asked with a glint of humor in her eyes.

She sounded so much like a black woman that if Jack had closed his eyes he wouldn't have been able to tell the difference. He nodded his head. He couldn't help letting his eyes roam her full figure. She was thick, with a fat ass so wide that you could see it from the front. Her green eyes sparkled with some kind of feminine mischief as she looked at him, almost daringly flirting with him, as if sizing him up. Her eyes strolled across his gear and then the lump in his pants from the gun.

"You got the right place. Come on in," she said, opening the door wide.

Jack glanced over his shoulder, adjusted his stride and casually walked in. He thought he smelled the faint aroma of weed. He tried not to stare, but couldn't help it. She was stacked like a brick house, with sharp curves all the way down to her sculptured calves. Her large pineapple-sized breasts jutted forward and her strawberry nipples hardened, like tiny faces watching him through the thin material of her wife beater. Her stomach was rippled with feminine muscles. A navel ring pierced her belly. Over her wide hips, she had on a pair of short shorts, the kind that mostly white girls wear, with the stringy threads hanging everywhere, the top button undone.

Jack tried not to look at the fat pussy print that was so big that it would be a shame to call it a monkey. It looked more like she had a gorilla in her panties. He continued to watch her. With a delicate finger, she pushed a ringlet of curly blond hair from her forehead. With that movement her soft breasts jiggled, straining against the sheer, thin fabric. She shifted positions from one leg to the other. For some unknown reason, Jack's mouth watered.

She was checking him out, too. As usual, Jack was rocking the latest gear – a Sean John suede jacket with matching baggy pants outfit, a pinky ring and a simple platinum chain that hung down to his stomach. Underneath his New York baseball cap he wore a black doo rag.

"Have a seat," Georgia Mae said with a smile. "Rasheed and Monique stepped out for a minute. You know tomorrow is the NBA draft, plus Fire is scheduled to fly to California."

"Damn, that's right!" Jack said as he tore his eyes away from the white girl's body as it suddenly occurred to him who she was.

Jack snapped fingers trying to recall her name. "Your name is ah, ah …"

"Georgia Mae," she said with a curt smile.

He frowned at her. She knew what he was thinking, so be-fore he could ask she said, "… but you can call me Game."

"Game," he repeated.

"Yup." She turned and slowly walked away, tossing her wide hips from side to side, ass shaking like jelly.

Jack grimaced, "Gotmuthafuckindamit," he muttered under his breath.

One side of her shorts rode way up the crack of her butt. It looked like she was wearing a partial thong as she moved across the room, causing a miniature earthquake. The motion in her ocean made Jack's eyes bulge. He also noticed the patch on the back of her head.

Suddenly, she turned around, catching him watching her. A lock of unruly hair fell over her eyes. She arched her foot on her toe and looked as if she wanted to ask him something. Her look was untamed, almost wild in a sexy kind of way.

"You want something to drink?" she asked in a throaty voice with a smirk on her face, the way a woman looks when she's loving every minute of a man checking her out.

"Yo, you can get me a beer," Jack said with a hard voice, trying to play it off.

He knew he needed to stay focused. He had come to ask a favor of Rasheed. Jack had been so busy the past few days that he had forgotten about the draft. Jack also wondered why Rasheed had not told him the girl was staying with Monique.

He sat down on the couch as a roach crawled across the floor in front of him. On the wall hung a Malcolm X photo with Malcolm pointing an angry finger, his top lip slightly curled with disdain. Jack shifted the gun in his pants to a comfortable position and reached for the PlayStation on the table. He noticed the half burnt blunt in the ashtray as Game sashayed back into the room with drinks in her hand.

Jack forbade his eyes to look in between her legs as she stood in front of him. He pretended to be interested in the game.

She set his drink down. Her per fume was a strange kind of musky sweetness. He sucked in a deep breath and let out a small sigh. She was standing too damn close. It felt like her nearness was suffocating him as he felt her eyes on him.

"Yo, how long have they been gone?" he asked for the sake of conversation.

His mind had already convinced him it was time to leave. Jack was faithful to Gina. Besides, he didn't do white chicks, period!

Game padded over to the loveseat and sat down, crossing her long legs, one over the other, Indian style. "They've been gone a couple of hours." She took a sip from her drink, eyeing him over the rim of her glass. "You smoke? I got some skunk weed. That's it in the ashtray, or if you like I can roll you a fresh one."

Jack looked up at her, tempted to take her up on her offer, but decided against it. "Naw, I'm good. I gotta bounce anyway."

Game fidgeted and stirred her drink with a manicured red fingernail as the ice clinked with the glass. "Psss ... what's up with all you good lookin' black guys? Got a sista on lockdown, smokin' on the solo. Chile, pah-leez, wha' da world comin' to?" Game sassed, rolling her eyes like she was dead serious.

Jack found himself smiling at her antics. She sounded so much like a black girl that he looked at her amazed. "What, you raised around blacks all yo' life or some shit?"

Game tossed her mane of hair over her shoulder and pushed her breasts forward. "Yeah, I was raised around blacks. I'm black. Trust me, Jack, you wouldn't know the difference with the lights off." She gave him a slight grin. A thin mustache of beer ringed her top lip. Jack burst out laughing. She smiled, too.

He stopped playing the game and looked at her closely, like it was his first time really seeing her. She caught him off-guard by calling him by name.

"You know my name?" he asked with a raised brow.

This time it was her turn to smile during the exchange of words. Purposely, she let the moment linger, while secretly enjoying the attention he was giving her. She took a sip from her drink and pursed her lips. "Saw your picture in the photo album over there." She pointed. "It looked like you was in jail posing with all them tattoos on your arms. You were cute, so I asked my girl Fire who you were."

"Fire?"

"Oops." She placed her hand over her mouth and giggled. "I mean Monique. Fire was her stage name."

"Damn, that's right. Both y'all used to dance before—"

"Nope, I'm still a dancer," she confirmed.

Playfully, Jack corrected her. "You're a scripper," he said, pronouncing "stripper" like the rapper Lil Jon.

"Whateeevah!" she said, snaking her neck from side to side, giving him her bent wrist with a sweep of her hand and a snap of her fingers.

They both laughed. She was mad stupid. Jack reached for the partial blunt in the ashtray as she stood up on wobbly legs and pulled her shorts out of her crotch. Jack shook his head. Onething he had to admit, she damn sure had a bangin' body.

Foolishly, he heard his voice say, "All scrippers have a cer-tain dance move. What's yours?"

"I don't know 'bout all the dance moves, but I can do a trick or two with my anus. Heard it drives the guys wild. You wanna see it?" she asked like a challenge, again turning the tables on him with her quick wit.

He was completely at a loss for words. "You got a girlfriend, Jack?"

"Yeah, I got a shorty." Just the thought of Gina brought him back to his senses. "She been down with a nigga for a minute."

Game noticed the change come over his face like the sun coming out from behind the clouds. Jack's mind drifted back to Gina, his down-ass chick. Jack shook his head and glanced at his watch. In doing so, his mind was released from the thought of her and when he glanced up, Game was standing over him with her coochie in his face. In the dim light, her olive skin seemed to radiate and glow.

For the first time he noticed the tiny pubic hairs climbing up her belly, looking like a golden spider web.

"Yo, a nigga gotta blaze up outta here," Jack said, looking up to see the now sour expression on her face. He saw something else, too, something he would later regret he did not recognize.

Somehow, again, it felt like she had inched closer. Her per-fume mingled in his nostrils. Her pink, pointed nipples swayed with her movement as she reached out and touched his arm. Fiery hot, he fought the urge to pull away from her. It felt as if somehow she was seeping into his soul like liquid fire. With her milky white skin against his brown skin, they looked at each other as the moment stalled like giant hands on a clock, only it was her hand on him.

"Aw, man, don't go," she pouted with petulant lips. "Ra-sheed and Fire will be back in a minute. I've been cooped up in this joint for the past two weeks, bored. I got some pizza in the fridge, got mo' beer and whatever else you want. Please stay." She rubbed her hand up and down his arm.

"A'ight!" He pulled away. "Yo, but only for a minute."

He was glad she had taken her hand off of him. He glanced down between her thighs. She was fat as a muhfuh. A smile appeared on her face as she picked up his empty glass.

"Hey, you like sports?" she asked out of the blue, causing Jack to slightly tilt his head as smoke from the blunt filtered the air like a small cloud from his mouth into his nose—the sign of a real weed connoisseur. She continued, with three fingers of her hand inside her pocket, standing with her hips leaning to one side.

"Well, in sports you got the first-string starters and the second string, just in case one of the players gets hurt." She looked at him with a hint of something written on her face. "I can play all positions when the first-string starter gets hurt." Her words hung in the air. "Only thing is, I can play my position much betta."

Jack wondered if she was talking about Gina being hurt. He took a long drag off the blunt, gagged and frowned as he licked his dry lips, looking at her through the smoke and haze. For some reason, his lips were numb and so was the tip of his tongue. He had been smoking all day and night. One thing was for sure, he needed to get something straight with this fly-ass white chick. She was nice on the scale of dime pieces, but he was not tryin' to cut. He cleared his throat and took another puff of the blunt. For some reason his lungs were hungry for the weed that numbed his mouth.

"Dig, Ma, no disrespect, know what I mean, but a nigga loyal to the wifey, plus I don't do white chicks."

Game's neck jerked back as her eyes narrowed at him.

"Uhmph!" she muttered, like he had just hit her in the chest with his fist. Somehow she managed to keep her composure. Placing her right hand on her hip, she looked at him. "I guess since you don't do white girls you don't do cocaine either? That's white and it makes you feel good, too."

"Hell, naw. I don't fuck wit' that shit! It's for suckers," Jack said as he took another long toke off the blunt and held the roach between his fingers.

Game grinned at him like a real vixen.

I got a trick or two for his ass, she thought as she watched him greedily suck on the blunt laced with coke. She spun on her heels with a mischievous look and strutted out of the room. Once in the kitchen, Game peered around the corner back into the living room. Jack was rolling a blunt with his face twisted to the side. He was trying to chase the white girl, cocaine, that had invaded his body and left him craving her.

She began crushing two white Ecstasy pills to put into Jack's drink. One pill was enough to stimulate the body, making a person experience a kind of ultra-sensitivity, a sensation like the body was one big orgasm. But two pills could be more than dangerous, depending on the individual's temperament. Not only could the drug enhance the sex drive, but it could do the same thing for rage if a person wasn't used to it.

Little did she know that Jack Lemon was the wrong nigga to be fucking with. When it came to rage, a quick death was better than feeling his wrath. Her back was to the door as she poured the crushed pills into his drink. The only thing going through her mind was what she was going to do to him—maybe even show him the trick she could do. She smiled as she thought about her coochie in his face.

As she made sure all of the powder was in his beer, she swirled it around with her finger. "So, you don't do white chicks, huh," she said to herself. "We'll see."

"What you doin'?" Jack asked, scaring the shit out of her. She spilled some of the substance on the counter as she flinched. As she turned around her breasts stood at attention with her nipples aiming at him as she held onto the edge of the counter. Her breath was lost in her throat.

For some reason she focused on the knife mark on Jack's neck from where he had been cut before.

"What you doin'?" Jack asked again, this time with more authority in his voice.

"I ... I ... I'm fixing you a drink," Game stuttered, her heart fluttering like a caged bird was inside of it.

She turned back around within the limited space between them. She quickly retrieved their drinks and passed him his. He took a step back and looked between her and the drink like he knew something was up.

"Let me find out you got some shit wit' 'cha." He eyed her carefully as his tongue danced around in his mouth the way coke heads do.

Game suddenly realized that her scandalous ways could fi-nally catch up with her. Now, fearfully, she watched as he held the drink up to the light, studying it.

"You think you tried a nigga, huh?" Jack spit, looking be-tween her and the glass.

Game had already made her mind up – she was going to kick Jack in the balls and make a run for the door. She braced herself as he stared at her.

"I thought you said you had pizza," Jack reminded, his now chapped lips curled into a smile. He swallowed hard against his cotton mouth. "A nigga got the munchies and that bomb-ass weed got me jonesin' for mo'."

With that said, he turned up the glass and guzzled the beer.

Yeah, just like that, she thought to herself as she watched him intently, just like Eve did Adam after she was tricked by the serpent and then watched dude take a bite out that piece of fruit. A tiny dribble of Heineken dribbled from the corner of his mouth down to his chin. She resisted the urge to wipe it with her fingers as her hungry eyes watched his handsome face like he was her prey and she was a lioness about to pounce.

With a satisfied smirk she stepped closer, smiled and mas-saged her breasts seductively as she swayed her hips over to the refrigerator. She bent over to show him her assets and give him the "home of the gorilla with all this pussy in your face" pose. The life of a stripper had more than its share of advantages.

She turned, doing the same dick-teasing move at the stove. With each move her scanty clothes seemed to be more revealing. Jack now stood with a full erection. Just that quickly the drug was starting to take effect, or maybe it was her? The front of his pants looked like a large tent as he moved his jaw from side to side, his tongue slightly hanging out. He suddenly had this overwhelming urge to grind his teeth. Shit was crazy. The good weed was starting to take effect on him, or so he thought. His body and mind were starting to experience a slight tingling sensation.

He noticed that Game's shoulder strap was pulled down, exposing the soft, milky-white flesh of her breasts. Jack turned the empty glass up to his lips, he saw the powdery substance at the bottom of the glass. He felt the effects of something powerful invading his body like an electrical current. He shook his head and slightly staggered. It felt like a hundred soldiers were marching through his veins and a million angry voices screamed, "Kill the bitch!"

For some reason, only now could he read the deception in her green eyes as she stood before him, pants lower than he could remember, pubic hairs long and blond, now showing the forest, land of the gorilla.

She saw him look at the glass, forehead wrinkled, frowning. Something was smoldering in his eyes as his jaw worked from side to side, teeth grinding, rage stirring.

Jack took a step forward, drew his hand back as far as he could and slapped the shit out of her. He hit her so hard that her neck snapped back causing her hair to fall into her face.

"Bitch, you put something in my muthafuckin' drink!" he yelled, taking a step forward, fist balled up. The millions of voices in his head all chanted in unison, "Kill her, beat that bitch like a man. Kill her!"

She had taken him to the point of no return. It felt like he was having an out-of-body experience. She had a large red welt on her face from his hand. She huffed as her breasts swelled defiantly, teeth streaked with blood.

She said boldly, "All I wanted was for you to fuck me! So I put X in your drink."

Jack, blinded with rage, couldn't hear anything she said. He drew back to punch her with his fist. She was pinned between him and the kitchen table. On the table was a large butcher knife.

"If you like, you can hit me again. Punish me," she said as blood dripped from her mouth.

Jack thought about all the tales he had heard about the drug X while he was in the joint. He had heard about the crazy maniac effect it had on chicks, but this shit was too crazy. To his amazement the white girl tore off the wife beater and her large, pendulous breasts flung free. Her small nipples were erect and pink. Tan marks outlined the contours of her breasts.

Next she stepped out of her shorts and white thong. Her vagina was so furry that it looked like she was trying to conceal a kitten between her thighs. She fell to her knees and unzipped his pants. Jack stood as if paralyzed, both fists balled up so tightly that his knuckles cracked. The bitch was past being bold. He had never experienced a woman like her in his entire life.

Somehow, unabashed, unrestrained, he took his gun out just as she bugged at the size of his dick, its length, its long, black, coiling thick veins. She could hardly get her hands around its girth. Her eyes grew wide. His dick was so dark it was like black-blue in contrast with her fair skin. It was as long as a small child's arm, but thicker. She stroked him up and down like a plunger, making the pre cum gleam in the head like pearls in a clamshell. She primed her lips with her tongue.

He raised the gun to her head, pulled the hammer back. She glanced up, didn't even bat an eye as she opened her mouth wide, taking him in her throat. She had to stretch her mouth so wide it felt like she was going to get lockjaw.

Jack couldn't help it, his mind was gone to that place of no return. He had to humiliate her, hurt her, bad! Violently he shoved his dick down her throat, making her gag and choke as he grabbed a handful of her hair, pressing the gun to her temple.

"Punk-ass bitch! Dis what you want, huh?" Jack yelled with his top lip curled to the side.

The drug had completely seized his body. Beads of sweat were starting to glisten on his forehead like shimmering brown gold as he continued to mash her head into his crotch, forcing his way down her throat. As he looked down at her through the fog of his mind, it looked like the more he dogged her out, the more she sucked on his dick, gagging and choking, saliva dripping off his penis onto her fingers and down his balls. Black and white skin, the combination a lethal curse, like the taboo, black blood with white.

"Shoot her! Shoot her!" the voices in his head exhorted as he held the gun to her head, forcing himself down her throat.

Somehow in the frenzied dual, amidst the loud slurping sounds that seemed to echo, Game masterfully contracted the muscles in her throat as she took him in deeper, almost all eleven, thick inches as he humped her face. Now she was the aggressor. Her head bobbed up and down so fast, so deep, so hot. Jack's eyes rolled to the back of his head. He was losing himself, losing control to her tempo.

Jack felt his knees grow weak. Absentmindedly, he placed the gun down on top of the stove. His eyes peeled open wide as she worked the juices in her mouth like some dance theme. Her tongue roamed up and down the ridge of his dick, while her lips trailed not far behind. Her mouth, succulent, moist, hot and wet, molested his organ, savoring every hypersensitive, tingling inch of him. It was three against one – lips, mouth and tongue, against his tool.

Jack heard a grunt, loud and bestial, like a wounded wild animal, then a moan that segued into a protracted groan. To his utter surprise, the sound was coming from deep within his throat, somewhere in the pit of his gut. He threw his head back and roared, opening his mouth wider.

Spasms rocked his body, then a shudder. He felt chills run up and down his spine as Game's hot mouth worked him, pushing him past the brink of ecstasy.

The fuckin' dope had completely possessed him. He was about to cum down her throat and somehow the white girl knew it, sensed it. On her knees Game smiled with the huge black dick in her mouth. He reached down and pulled her up by her hair. Her mouth was still agape in awe and shock as she screeched in pain.

His was dick dangling with a long string of cum seeping out of the head. Her large breasts bounced, swinging in front of him. Jack furrowed his brow when he saw cum, like honey, sparkling in the hairs of her vagina in the gap between her wide thighs. A line of cum ran down her inner thigh. Jack could have sworn he saw a glint of a smile tug at Game's lips.

Deep down, something about her infuriated him. Now he just wanted to dog this bitch out. She stood before him, unafra-id, unrestrained and untamed. Perhaps it was the drugs, or the fact that she had tried a nigga big time, putting that shit in his drink.

He grabbed her by the shoulders, spinning her around so hard that her hair twirled like an umbrella. He bent her over the table, forcing her head down, ass up. He spread her legs. She muttered something as she tried to look back over her shoulder. He slammed her head down hard on the table. She whimpered a dove's cry with her butt and furry pussy tooted up in the air. She had a forest down there, home of the gorilla.

"So you want me to fuck you, huh?" Jack said with a menacing scowl on his face, eyes ablaze with fury that he would later regret.

He stroked himself long and hard, pointed his dick between her ass cheeks, intending to do serious damage. He couldn't help but admire her luscious backside. Like the Devil, the dope told him to. Bent over like she was, Jack slapped her hard on the ass, leaving a handprint. She cried out in pain and tried to raise her head. He slammed it back down on the table with a loud thud.

Jack was deranged. Now his intent was to abuse her body by violently taking her from the back, in more ways than one. He spit on his hand, rubbed it up and down his long shaft, and aimed it as he grabbed a handful of her flesh, spreading her cheeks, opening the pink morsel of flesh dripping wet with her juices like dew on a watermelon.

He eased inside her. Slowly she wiggled her ass in an attempt to accommodate him. Once he got the mushroom-like head of his dick in her tight vagina he rammed it in, eight inches, causing her to cry out in pain. She looked back at him and for the first time she had pure torment written on her face. He went deeper, giving her his full length.

She screamed to the top of her lungs, thrashed and bucked. "You're hurting me!" she screeched, pleading. "Go slow. Ohhh …"

She reached back with her hand. He slapped it down and thrust deeper into her.

"Oh, oh, shit, yo … yo … you black motherfucker!"

Game was talking like a white woman now as Jack continued to fervidly pound away inside her guts. The table shook so hard that it felt like the legs were about to fall off.

Sweat poured off both of their bodies as his balls banged against her.

She could feel him deep within, like he was rubbing against her ribs. He was frantic, like a raving maniac out of control. With each of his powerful thrusts the table continued to slam against the wall as she cried out for him to stop. He had the pussy on fire.

"Oh …You killiiing mee!" she pleaded.

It only seemed to bring more of the animal out of him. Now for the first time, she was concerned for her health. Jack only ignored her as he continued to grunt and fuck her from the back, making her pussy pop.

Finally, about an hour later, he stopped and pulled out of her. She was red, irritated and sore. Soon as he withdrew his dick, her pussy farted long and hard. He squirted cum all over her back and hair. They were both winded, their breath echoing like chants of a song that neither of them had rehearsed.

"Naw bitch, you gonna rememba dis dick," he hissed, standing behind her.

He reached for the Crisco cooking oil on the stove and squeezed oil between her ass and all over her back, his dick in his hand like a large battering ram. He looked down at the small hole of her anus. If the Bible mentioned something about a camel and the eye of a needle, then surely his dick could go through something the size of a dime.

With his lubricated finger, he eased it inside of her ass. To his amazement, Game jacked up one ass cheek, then the other, and spread her thick round ass wide, making it jiggle and bounce at the same time. The little pink hole in the center slightly winked at him as it opened like "open-sesame."

Jack did a double-take, blinking his eyes, like what the fuck?

Then his mind flashed back to what she had said earlier about being able to do a trick or two with her anus. He placed the head of his pipe inside of her, determined to do as much damage as humanly possible.

Game took a deep breath, eased off the side of the table, bent all the way down, touched the floor with her hands, and made some kind of noise that Jack could not make out.

He glided an inch or two inside of her. She groaned, he moaned and slipped in deeper. She raised her head, looking back at him. The tight sensation that was gripping him suddenly made him lose control. He knew it had to be the drug. He plunged deep inside of her.

She let out a shriek as her hands reached back to block some of the length of his penetration. He was building momentum, like riding down a mountain. His pace quickened. Jack rode her long and hard. She knew that he was trying to punish her. He had the right idea, but the wrong woman. Together, they reached multiple climaxes, her breasts swinging back and forth as his body clapped against hers. She bit down on her lip, taking all of him. He pound ed away inside of her with deep, long strokes. He had never fucked a chick in the ass before in his life.

Finally, they came together like two desperate people run-ning a race, a fuck marathon. In the end, they both were drenched with sweat, panting. He pulled his dick out of her, leaving a swollen, irritated gaping hole the size of a small fist.

Jack looked at his watch, 4:24 a.m. His dick was still rock hard!

Game turned around and looked at him as she wiped her clit and made a face that stayed that way as she continued to feel around down there.

So many things were going through Jack's mind. He had failed miserably at punishing the white girl with his dick. For some reason, the drug made him stay bad-tempered, evil like the Devil.

"Bitch, I should kill your punk ass," Jack said.

Game continued to rub her clit like it was on fire as she glared at him with dried blood on her chin. She responded tersely, "You already killed me. You killed the poonaney."

Jack frowned at her and her slick-ass mouth. They were both high off X and still horny as hell.

"Spend the night. You know you want to," Game said, looking at his dick, which was still hard and swinging from side to side.

She was right, the drug made him want to take her again. Instead, he walked over to the faucet and drank some water with his hands, thirsty like a homeless dog. She watched him with her thick legs spread and continued to rub her clit. It dawned on him just how freaky this white bitch was, for he had done his damnedest to punish her. He slapped the shit out of her, roughhoused the pussy and unsuccessfully tried to molest her asshole.

The bitch must have loved every minute of him sodomizing the shit out of her. For a second, a voice in his head chanted, "Strangle the bitch! Strangle the bitch!"

Jack took a step forward, teeth grinding, hands coiling, mus-cles tensing. He recoiled his fingers like claws, staring at the soft white fleshy tissue on her neck. His palm print was still on her face from where he had slapped her.

"W-w-why you looking at me like that?" Game asked, taking a tentative step back.

This shit is crazy, Jack thought. The dope was making him crazy. The bold, crazy-ass white bitch standing before him nude still rubbing her coochie with cum running down her leg was crazy. His fucking throat was so dry, his mouth was numb and why in the hell was he grinding his fucking teeth so damn much? It felt like he was going to crack them. His dick was so hard he had to shove it into his pants, but it had a mind of its own and didn't want to cooperate. Fuckin' dope! He grabbed his gun and turned to walk away, feeling like a nigga that tried to play, but had gotten played instead.

Then, for some dumb reason, he heard his mouth say, "I thought you said Rasheed and Mo was comin' back in a few?"

She rolled her eyes and sucked her teeth. Why is he still asking about them? she thought.

Game took a step closer, one of her eyes was slightly red, and her hair was matted to her forehead with sweat. She placed her hand on the curve of her wide hip as she turned her leg outward.

"I lied to you. They ain't comin' home tonight. They staying at a hotel." Then Game added, like some practiced cliché, "You know you comin' back for mo'. Look at the bulge in your pants," she said, pointing and taking a step forward. "You said you don't do white girls or coke. Well, two white girls name coke and Game just did 'cha." She chimed. "Touché!"

"What?" Jack grumbled as it dawned on him what the bitch had just said.

He balled his fist up tight and took a step forward, fully in-tent on dropping her like a man. He went to swing, but she just stood there with her perfect white, feral teeth showing, rubbing her clit as she looked at him like a sex fiend. Jack unclenched his fist and turned to walk out the door. The cackle of her laughter followed him.

From that day forward, Jack would never get high off any-thing but life. The white girl had taught him a lesson. And not just that, he went up in her raw. Fuckin' drugs!

Ten

The Family

Jack parked Gina's Jeep in the front yard of Grandma Hat-tie's house. The yard was cluttered with cars. Across the street was a Channel Five news van. Two crackheads strolled by as Jack hopped out of the Jeep, giving them the screwface, like don't even think about stealing shit out this yard. The junkies quickly focused their attention on the white woman and the two news reporters inside the van. They were obviously on the wrong side of town, but if it was announced that Rasheed Smith was drafted into the NBA, the reporter would rush the house for a story.

Jack walked inside the house. It was jam-packed with folks. The mood was festive. He saw cats he hadn't seen in ages, chicks, too. The television volume was turned up loud on SportsCenter.

Rasheed sat perched in the middle of the couch as people mingled about all around him. He looked like a zombie with both hands nervously holding a forty ounce of malt liquor.

"Damn, nigga, you look like shit!" Rasheed said to his man Jack.

It was the truth. Jack had been up all night and was still horny and extremely thirsty, still wired from the X pills. It felt like his jaws were cemented together. Jack ignored his friend's remark as he stared at the forty in his hands. For some unknown reason his right eye kept twitching. Jack sat down next to Rasheed.

Rasheed took one look at Jack's chapped lips and frowned. He then sniffed the air and leaned away from Jack. He was about to say something, but Jack spoke first.

"Nigga, why didn't you tell me dat white bitch was staying at Monique's?" Jack asked with a snarl.

"Georgia Mae?"

"Yeah, Game," Jack said.

"Why … how you know?" Rasheed asked with a little too much concern in his voice. "It wasn't important. What, you met her? She's dope, huh?" Rasheed said with a smile that conveyed more than appreciation for her.

The sportscaster started talking. J.T., from high school, started talking louder. "You know Rasheed ain't in the first round because of racism."

Someone else shouted, "But the rest of the players are mostly black."

"That only makes it worse. Why they only got mostly black dudes?" J.T. asked stupidly, staggering across the room.

"Hey!" J.T. yelled, looking around trying to find the culprit who threw a magazine at him.

"Sit your dumb ass down!" a voice yelled from amongst the crowd.

Everyone laughed as J.T. did just that.

As Rasheed sat on the couch nervous, with butterflies the size of bats in his stomach, his mind flashed back to the last game of the year, the AAA Championship game that he had played in against the Spartans. The big game that the coach had been preparing him for, the game of his life, the one that would help decide whether or not he would go pro. It seemed like everyone who had something to do with sports in New York had been in the house. The media was there in full blast; even a couple of basketball stars and their agents came out to watch the big game.

The entire first quarter, the opposing team was guarding him with two and three men. The defense was good. They kept changing it up. Finally, he was able to get a shot off—air ball. He missed everything. Running down court, the white boy, his opponent, shoved him and he fell hard. He looked up at the coach and the man was screaming at him. Them white boys was laying some serious wood. By halftime he had no points, and not just that, the opposing team managed to keep him off the boards—no rebounds. The referees refused to give him any calls. It was a game played at the opposing team's school.

At halftime in the locker room, Coach Jones screamed so much that he became hoarse. Rasheed was embarrassed. In his heart, he knew that he was scared because of all of the pressure. It caused him to not just let himself down, but his teammates, too. They couldn't even look him in the eye. The Spartans were all white boys and regardless of what anyone said, them white boys could play some ball. They played rough and hard.

Finally, the coach turned to Rasheed, the team captain. "Maybe this isn't your team or your game. A true champion welcomes a challenge. That's the only thing that separates him from the rest, shows if he's the best. None of you deserve to go to the pros," the coach said angrily. Everyone in the locker room knew who the statement was really directed toward.

Rasheed rose to his feet so fast that the towel on his lap fell two feet in front of him. "Yo, I got this! We gotta start playing together like a team. Y 'all standing around watching me! Move! Set some picks!" Rasheed looked at his coach. "Set some plays for me. Get me the damn ball in the post!" The coach grinned at the hyper-charged attitude of his player. The art of good coaching was knowing how to motivate the players.

Rasheed's team, the Wild Cats, started the second half off sixteen points behind the opposing team. The crowd was going wild. Rasheed saw Magic Johnson in the stands. Just like he had asked, the coach ran plays for him. Rasheed missed his first three shots with the lanky white boys guarding him. As he hustled down court, the coach gave him a pained expression as he yelled for another player off the bench to replace Rasheed. This was it, the biggest game of his entire life and he couldn't produce.

Rasheed refused to come out of the game and mouthed to coach, "No."

The coach shook his head, making a face at Rasheed that he was disappointed with his game. Rasheed stole a pass and ran the ball all the way up the court and pulled up in the white boy's face, hit a three – all net, and was fouled. The crowd booed.

Rasheed went to the line and for the first time that day, he talked shit to the white boys just like he did on the Brooklyn basketball courts. He was in his zone as he shot the free throw. He went on to score twenty-two points in the second half. He was hot, hitting fifteen straight points, and now with six seconds left in the game, they were down by one.

The coach called a screen. Rasheed would come off his man and roll to the free throw line for a pass. It worked as planned. As his teammate passed him the ball, Rasheed pulled up for the shot and was fouled. He went to the free throw line knowing he could either tie the game by hitting one free throw or lose the game if he missed both.

There were two seconds left on the game clock. Rasheed knew he was a seventy percent shooter from the line.

A piece of cake, he told himself as he dribbled the ball twice.

Bend your knees, use your wrist, deep breath...

Swoosh!

The first shot sailed through the net. The score was now tied. Rasheed released a deep breath that he didn't even know he was holding.

The boisterous crowd had gotten louder. They were stomp-ing their feet, waving orange flags and other paraphernalia in front of him. A fan was actually standing a few feet in back of the basketball goal yelling at him.

Rasheed glanced over at the bench. Some of his teammates were holding hands huddled together. A few were actually on their knees with their hands clasped in front of them. All wore solemn faces, especially the coach. He had a towel in his mouth, gnawing on it. The future of this team rested on Rasheed's shoulders.

The ball left his hand as if in slow motion – a surreal mo-ment. The world had slowed to a crawl as everyone held their breath. The ball hit the rim, bounced high, bounced ... bounced ...falling out of the rim.

To everybody's amazement, Rasheed came flying high above the rim over everyone on the floor. With one hand, he palmed the ball and did a ferocious one-hand dunk with his nuts in the seven foot center's face! The clock shrilled! The game was over! His teammates went wild! They stormed the court, burying him with emotional hugs. They had won the championship game. For the first time ever they had made the front page of the "USA Today" sports section.

Now Rasheed sat in front of the television. Nervous couldn't begin to describe what he was feeling. He was past that, almost to the point of being frantic.

Jack sat next to him grinding his teeth. He wasn't about to tell Rasheed about how Game had stunted on him by pulling that bullshit with the dope. Plus, everyone knew that he didn't mess with white chicks.

"I stopped by y'all's crib. Mmmm, uh, why you got that cracka broad stayin' with y'all?" Jack asked, raising his voice above the crowd in the room.

Rasheed wasn't really paying any attention to him though. J.T. was drunk and dancing in front of the television.

"Move, nigga!" Rasheed yelled. "Me and Mo went to a hotel last night. In a few days she's leaving for Cali." Then he smiled. "So, you met Georgia Mae. She's dope, huh?" Rasheed said with a sly smile.

Jack was thinking, she's dope alright, but he could sense something else was going on.

"Gina's been asking about you. Said you was supposed to come back last night."

Just then, the kitchen door opened. Grandma Hattie ap-peared, followed by Monique, Aunt Esta, Gina and a few more women that Jack didn't recognize. They all had trays of soul food – collard greens, fried chicken and barbecue ribs.

Gina hobbled so badly that Jack had to resist the urge to get up and help her. Besides, his conscience was getting to him. Not to mention, the dope still had him dry-mouthed and horny.

Gina's long hair was in a ponytail with curls hanging on each side of her face. She wore a white sundress with flowers, looking like the average attractive black woman. As she looked at Jack her eyes sparkled and a light smile tugged at her cheeks. Her cinnamon complexion seemed to glow. One of the women turned and whispered something, causing all the women to erupt in giddy laughter, an indication of the jovial mood in the old house.

Suddenly the bright smile on Gina's face froze as her eyes narrowed looking at Jack. He rose to greet her, genuinely happy to see his woman. The room was full of noisy chatter as he bopped over and kissed Gina on the cheek with his dry chapped lips. He continued to grind his teeth as he tried to speak. Gina reached out and pinched him hard, grabbing a fold of his skin underneath his shirt.

"Ouch!" Jack screeched.

"Nigga, where you been?" she demanded with a frown on her face so intense that Jack took a step back, at the same time trying to remove his tongue from the roof of his mouth. The room suddenly was dead quiet as the announcer began to call the first name in the draft. No one was paying any attention to Jack and Gina.

"You had them same clothes on yesterday. And look at you, what's wrong with your face and shit?" Gina said, pulling on his shirt.

She peered closer, sniffed him to pussy check, the way a woman does when she's on the verge of going the fuck off, searching for another female's scent or any other evidence. The rowdy crowd in the front room yelled as a picture of Rasheed flashed across the screen, along with a few other athletes that the commentator said had a very slim chance of getting drafted.

"Nigga, you got me twisted if you think I don't know when something is up with you," Gina said.

"Chill, Ma, a nigga been on the grind tryna make shit hap-pen," Jack said, grinding his teeth and rubbing the spot where she had just pinched the shit out of him.

Grandma Hattie looked up at them as she wiped her hands on her apron. The thick creases in her forehead expressed concern. She ambled over. Her mahogany skin was lined so deep with age that some of her wrinkles overlapped each other. She knew they were fighting. Her weary mouth smiled, but her eyes didn't.

"Y'all be nice, you hear?" she said sweetly and then placed a comforting hand on Gina's shoulder. "She's much betta. Child still needs some rest, but you can take her home now. She done ate me outta house and home." Grandma Hattie laughed, causing Gina to smile at the old woman.

Jack just ground his teeth with an urge for a beer so bad it was driving him crazy. Grandma Hattie's expression changed as she shrugged her small narrow shoulders.

"Boy, you take good care of dis girl. All she needs is some rest and a lot of love now."

The old woman didn't tell Jack that, more than likely, Gina would walk with a limp for the rest of her life.

There was some commotion at the door. Everyone turned to see Lieutenant Brown walking through with two cases of beer. The noise level got even louder. A few women yelled out his name.

Drunken J.T. staggered. "Man, somebody give dis nigga a quarter or somethin'. How'd you know I was thirsty bro?" Everybody cracked up at J.T.'s crazy ass.

Brown smiled and walked past him in his royal blue sweat suit. His thick, curly hair shined as a glint of sunlight danced off of it. He spoke to everyone in the house, people who had known him most of his life. The females sang his name in chorus with a few flirtatious invitations. Shit, he was a prime catch as far as the ladies were concerned. He was good looking and had a job with benefits.

Rasheed looked up from the television as Anthony reached out his fist. "Good luck, dawg." Rasheed gave him a dap. For a moment, Rasheed thought about the man who used to be his mentor, how he had taken him to his first basketball game. A lot had changed since Anthony had started working for the beast. He stepped over a red fire truck Lil' Malcolm was playing with on the floor. He playfully ruffled the child's hair as he bent down to play with him, teetering with both cases of beer stacked under one arm.

In the dining room Gina stood stunned as she looked at the handsome cop. Her heart raced in her chest. A riot of emotions went off in her head as he walked straight toward her. The last time she had seen him she was busting caps at his dome and fleeing the scene of a double homicide with a bullet in her leg. Now she felt trapped. She would have run away, but she couldn't. She hadn't told Jack that he was the cop that she shot at. She didn't know his name until now.

Jack shuffled his feet as Anthony walked up and pecked Grandma Hattie on the cheek, causing the old woman to blush like a school girl. He then set the boxes of beer on the table as they exchanged pleasantries.

Anthony reached into one of the boxes and retrieved a can of beer as a woman walked over and said something to him. He ignored her and instead looked over at Jack and Gina. Embar-rassed, the woman grabbed a can of beer and walked away hoping nobody saw how she got played. The expression on Anthony's face changed like a dark shadow had washed over it.

Casually he strolled over, taking a drink from his beer. "You look so much like your father it's a damn shame," he said, shaking his head as he talked to Jack and sticking his fist out so Jack could gave him a dap.

Jack mopped his face with his weary hand, swallowed hard, trying not to stare at the beer. He had sworn to give up drinking and smoking. Game had taught him a lesson. Anthony then turned his attention to the pretty girl standing next to Jack. He remembered her being Jack's girl, but there was something about her that he just couldn't put his finger on. Her piercing green eyes held him, but there was something else.

"I'm still tryna figure out how my ole man ended up being a revolutionar y and you a cop."

Anthony was still looking at Gina when he spoke. "It's sim-ple. We were both pulled in two different directions to serve our people." He continued to stare at Gina, perplexed. Neither of them dared to break their optic standoff.

"Don't I ... know you from ..." Anthony said. The words trailed off his tongue like he was experiencing déjà vu.

Jack stood between the two of them and watched the verbal volley being exchanged as Brown furrowed his brow in an attempt to force his mind to remember something.

"Why you ain't at work today?" Grandma Hattie asked from the kitchen, sticking her head out the door.

The woman who was trying to get his attention earlier walked past Anthony, attempting to make eye contact. Jack watched as Anthony took another hearty drink of his beer and his mouth watered. That shit still had him buggin'. What the fuck they put in them damn pills? he wondered. He was grinding his teeth, except now it was getting worse. He was actually moving his jaw from side to side.

"I got suspended," Anthony said sourly.

Somehow Rasheed overheard that part of their conversation.

"I told 'cha them crackas don't care about a nigga when he work for the beast. You'd come out better being a slave catch-er."

Anthony made a face and moved his lips as if to speak then changed his mind. Jack rubbed at his throat and said he needed some cold water.

Gina tore her eyes away from the cop and glowered at Jack. "His ass been up to something," she mumbled under her breath.

Jack excused himself and walked off to the kitchen. He was dehydrated and then some. With Jack gone and everyone huddled around the television, it seemed like it was just the two of them, Gina and the cop. He could have reached out and touched the silky baby hair that cascaded down the side of Gina's face, he was standing just that close to her. In some ways he could also see the innocence in her youthful beauty. He could also see the hood in her as her ponytail hung over her shoulder onto her breast, partially concealing a tattoo.

"So, Mr. Po-po, what did you get suspended fo'?" Gina asked, smiling devilishly as she limped over to the chair and sat down with great difficulty.

Brown frowned as he watched her closely.

Gina smoothed the wrinkles out of her dress with the palms of her hand.

An image flashed through Brown's mind. "How did you hurt yourself?" he asked with his eyebrows bunched together. This was

now the detective in him talking.

"I was runnin' and I fell," Gina said, looking up at him with her hands still on her thighs. Her eyes matched his, almost inviting him to go along with the dialogue.

"Running from what?" Brown asked, never taking his eyes off the beautiful girl.

Secretly, Gina was enjoying the verbal sparring with the cop, all the while being conscious of the potential dangers that lurked like a deadly shark in knee-deep water.

"Didn't yo' momma teach you not to answer a question with a question?" Gina mimicked in a heavy New York accent that made Brown smile. "I'm saying, I asked you first. What was you suspended for?"

Brown pulled in his lips, thought for a second and reached over and pulled out a chair, straddling it backward.

"Excuse my language, but I was suspended for some bull-shit," he said bitterly as he sighed.

She could tell that he felt uneasy talking about it. In the next room it had grown even more quiet, as more names were being announced. Rasheed sat in front of the television chewing his thumbnail as Monique sat by his side, her face resembling his, the pain built up from the stress of the unknown. The once jubilant mood was now somber, coated in heavy silence like a funeral home parlor.

"I'm sure you've heard of the Death Struck case," Anthony said.

Gina shifted in her chair uncomfortably and stretched her legs, crossing one ankle over the other, catching Brown looking at her heart-shaped figure.

"No, I haven't," she lied with a straight face as she leaned forward in her chair expressing interest.

Anthony paused for a moment, apprehensive about telling her about the case.

Those eyes, he thought.

"Well?" she said, attempting to stir him out of his deep thoughts.

He then looked around and saw Rasheed and remembered everyone was there for him. He was amongst people he consi-dered family and she wouldn't be there, or even with Jack, if she weren't. He let his guard down and began speaking.

"Well, the disappearance of Damon Dice and the murder of his bodyguard have become very high profile cases. Not just in America, but all over the world. I didn't even know hip-hop was that big," Anthony said matter-of-factly, not telling her anything she didn't already know. "I have my suspicions who is behind it all but that's when I was pulled from the case and suspended."

"Really?" Gina asked, raising her eyebrows as she looked at him, pretending to be shocked. "It must be gang related or something," she said, trying to get more information from him. "You know, being a rapper and all."

"I don't think it's gang related," he said, dispelling that myth. "It's something deeper than that. I do know that it's just two people … for now."

"Two people? Why do you say that?"

"Just my instincts," he said, trying not to give more information than necessary. "I do know that it's a male and female."

"A girl?" she said innocently.

"Yeah, and I think I'm this close to catching her." He ges-tured with his thumb and forefinger.

"Her," she pointed and hunched her shoulders. "Why so much emphasis on the woman, if you say it's a man and a woman?"

"Of course, I would like to catch both of them, but it's the woman who's killed two men in cold blood and then tried to kill me. It's personal now."

"Sounds like you need to be careful. The next time she shoots at you she might not miss."

Brown jerked his neck back as his eyebrows shot up. "How did you know that she shot at me?" Brown asked with a stern expression on his face, catching her completely off-guard.

"Huh, mmm, I think I read about it somewhere."

"You just told me that you never heard about the case."

Playing with fire, Gina was about to get burned. Brown was now looking at her so absorbedly that he frightened her. As she sat in the chair in front of him, she could feel her heart pounding so hard in her chest that she was sure he could see it.

Jack entered the room from the kitchen. He had a tall glass of ice water in one hand and a greasy chicken wing in the other. His pants sagged so low that his Glock was showing in his drawers. As soon as he joined them, he looked at Gina and could sense that something was wrong.

"How long you been out the joint?" Anthony asked.

"Why, what you askin' for? This ain't cops and robbers day. Nigga, if you come as a friend, you askin' too many damn questions, know what I mean," Jack said as he continued to look back and forth between Anthony and Gina.

Anthony saw the big-ass Glock in Jack's pants and read the warning expression on his face.

Gina got up and walked into the next room. Jack followed as the female who had tried to strike up conversation earlier with Anthony walked back over and attempted to start another conversation with him. He never heard a word the woman said.

Rasheed stared at the television as Jack and Gina entered the room. The murmurs, muffled voices, and occasional giggles were now a scant reminder of the once festive mood. A few friends and family members had come, eaten the free food and drank the drinks, wished Rasheed good luck and left. Crazy-ass J.T. was cracking jokes about what it would be like if he were President. In all, the atmosphere now felt drained.

Rasheed looked as if the very life had been sucked out of him. A man's dreams are often all he has in the ghetto, a dream of getting out. When you take that away from him, you take away a part of the man.

Rasheed lowered his head, crestfallen, with his wide narrow shoulders slumped. Monique sat next to him and affectionately caressed the nape of his neck, cooing words of encouragement into her man's ear. A black woman's task is never easy.

They were announcing the final players who would be se-lected in the draft. The camera zoomed in on Isaiah Thomas, President of the New York Knicks basketball association. He looked into the camera with a stoic expression and reached down to open the envelope for the Knicks' final pick of the draft. Feeling defeated, Rasheed raised his head to look at the television.

Isiah announced with a slight smile on his face, "The New York Knicks would like to pick Rasheed Smith of the St. John Wild Cats. This year's AAA Champions."

The once somber room erupted in joyous clamor, with Mo-nique being the loudest. "Thank ya, Jesus! Thank ya, Jesus!"

She jumped around so much she re-injured her ankle. Eve-ryone was overcome with the kind of emotion that just fills you with beautiful euphoria as people celebrated in their own way.

As soon as she heard the noise, Grandma Hattie rushed out of the kitchen. Wiping her wet hands on her apron, she began to hobble over to Rasheed. He had pure shock written all over his face, as the reality of what had just happened started to come down on him. As Rasheed saw his grandmother nearing him, he stood and walked toward her.

Once they met, he began to cry in sobs that racked his body as he hugged the black woman who had raised him. He held her tightly as she began to cry, too. The tears streaked down his face. He was overcome with emotions that he could not describe. It was like waking up one day struggling to feed your family and the next, being able to buy your child nice shoes or send them to a good school to get an education, the things that white folks took for granted and that blacks constantly struggled for.

There was a loud knock on the door and in walked the me-dia, with lights so bright that they made Rasheed squint his eyes. A white woman shoved a microphone in his face and asked him to make a comment regarding being drafted right here, at home, by the New York Knicks. Lost for words, drunk-ass J.T. tried to take over the interview.

"I wanna give a shout out to all my niggas in the Tombs on lock down – Deemo, Tat Tat and dem."

While the reporters were in the house getting an interview, the crackheads were outside breaking into the news van.

Jack just looked on as he continued to grind his teeth, jaw clenching from side to side. He was elated that a nigga could eat and now feed his family, but there was one thing that Jack didn't like. Why was the nigga crying on national television? Niggas out of BK don't cry. A nigga too thorough for that soft shit, Jack was thinking.

From across the room, Anthony was watching, happy for Rasheed. Suddenly his cell phone rang. With all the commotion, he walked into the kitchen to take the call. To his surprise, it was Dr. Wong, the medical examiner. He talked urgently.

"I hear you got suspended," the doctor said in thickly ac-cented English. "If you can find time, I need see you down here at the morgue."

"About what?" Anthony questioned as he raised his voice above the crowd and placed his finger in his ear.

"Captain Brooks, the man you fight with, he is here."

"What?!"

"Not just that. Guess who else?"

"Who?"

"Your boss. They looking at Damon Dice's body."

"Shit! They found him?"

"Sort of," Wong replied.

"What the fuck you mean, sort of?"

"They found him in dump without his head."

"Decapitated?"

"Yep. Come by tonight. I have something for you might help you solve the case." With that, Dr. Wong hung up the phone.

Eleven

Lieutenant Brown

The Brooklyn morgue was located on the south side of town next to the old cemetery. It was surrounded by an ancient twelve-foot gate with spiked points. At night, the place looked like a haunted castle. When Brown arrived it was dark outside, heavy with dense patches of fog. Brown could barely see his hand in front of his face. The sound of his shoes echoed on the pavement as he briskly walked up the stairs.

At the entrance of the morgue sat two lion head statues, as if guarding the door. As Brown walked up to the door, he was startled by a black cat that hissed and drew back its lips to expose its sharp teeth. As it brushed by his leg, skirting down the stairs, Brown jumped out of the way just as Dr. Wong opened the door.

"See what you did to kitty," Wong chided with a smirk on his face. Wearing a stained white smock, he held a sandwich in his hand.

Brown made a face at Dr. Wong and replied, "Damn cat is as big as a fucking dog."

Dr. Wong blinked, squinting at Brown in inter vals. "Tom Cat big pussy. Maybe he no like you."

"Maybe I put bullet in ass," Brown retorted, mimicking Wong in broken English as he stepped inside the morgue.

Together they walked down the long corridor. The place was eerie, old and damp. They turned and walked into a room. Dr. Wong entered first and turned and waited for Brown. Every time he entered the room, it always reminded him of some type of death chamber, with its white porcelain autopsy tables that looked so old that they could have been donated to a science museum.

The air was stale, tinged with an awful smell—death. The room temperature was refrigerator cold. Modern equipment appeared to be non-existent. Brown looked at all the electrical autopsy saws. On the table he saw a body with a white paper sheet covering it. On the table across from it was another body zipped up in a gray body bag. From the corner of the body bag a white substance was dripping on the floor. No matter how many times Brown viewed mutilated dead bodies, all the senseless killings, it gave him the creeps. He never had the stomach for it.

Dr. Wong took a bite out of his sandwich and began to talk with his mouth full of food. "I show you something to help you with Death Struck case," he said as he swallowed hard. "Body under sheet belong to Tommy Knight, the man known as Big Prophet. I about to perform eyetopsee," he spoke, pronouncing the word "autopsy" wrong. "The other body," Wong pointed, "belong to Damon Dice."

Brown's jaw went slack and his eyes scrolled over to their corners as he looked over at the gray body bag. Damon Dice was in there, headless.

"Which one you wanna see first?" Wong asked, gesturing with the sandwich still in his hand.

Brown strolled over to Damon's body bag. With a slight nod, he indicated to Wong to open it.

Wong walked over and unzipped the bag with one hand. The bag fell away from the deceased body like a

A Gangsta's Bitch 2

husk. The horrible smell of rotten flesh was overwhelming. Brown took a step back, gagging as he placed a hand over his mouth. Wong took a bite out of his sandwich and walked over to a table and then came back. He passed Brown a face mask, which did little to help.

Wong finished off the remainder of his sandwich, walked over to the sink, washed his hands, and put on a pair of latex gloves. All the while Brown stood his distance, looking at the headless body. Maggots were crawling all over Damon's genital area and large bugs were so plentiful that you could scoop them up by hand.

Brown began to itch all over. He looked distressed as he scratched his neck.

"W ... w ... where did you find him?"

"Poor guy was at Brooklyn dump. One of the workers dis-cover him," Wong spoke. "As soon as prints came back identify the body, Chief Daniels and Captain Brooks and his men were all over the place." As Wong spoke, Brown continued to peer at Damon.

"So, my boss Chief Daniels is the one tipping off Brooks," Brown said, talking to himself.

"What you say?" Wong asked.

"Nothing."

"I called you because I overhear your boss mention your name. He say something 'bout a cab and a lady with blond wig. They say together they work on case like team to find cab company and woman. He tell Chief Brooks, as favor, he let him make arrest. They both agree to keep you off case."

"Damn, you overheard that?" Brown asked as he scratched his chest.

He should have figured it out, but he never would have thought it was his boss. That was truly fucked up. Now he wondered why they wanted him off the case. This was a high profile case, the kind that drew enough publicity to get a man promoted… or demoted. Brown watched and scratched like he had fleas as Dr. Wong examined the body.

"My bet is he had some kind of basilar skull fracture."

"A what?" Brown retorted.

"Trauma to the back of the head."

As Wong continued talking, Brown began to gag. "How in the hell can you say he had a skull fracture when he ain't got no head?" he said in a muffled voice as he scratched his neck.

Wong smiled with food stuck between his crooked teeth. "I say dat because there is blood in the airway. It's only one way that could have happened. Blood dripped down the back of the throat while he was breathing."

"You mean, he was alive when his head was cut off?"

Wong nodded his head.

"Damnit!" Brown exclaimed as he now scratched his jaw and took a timid step back from Wong. He had maggots crawling up his sleeve and his gloves were covered with them.

"I'm not sayin' he was conscious. He had a blood pressure, even if slight."

Brown couldn't take it anymore. He turned away from the sight of the decapitated body and momentarily shut his eyes as he inhaled the horrible rancid smell of death.

After Wong washed his hands and changed his gloves, he walked over to Big Prophet's body. He pulled the sheet back, exposing the badly burned corpse.

"Sho' you somethin'. You eva watch eyetopsee before?" he asked and pointed to Big Prophet's chest.

The markings were still visible, like a dead man talking from the grave, trying desperately to tell who his killer is. With his fingernail, Prophet had scratched initials that looked like "7C". The markings were unintelligible. As Brown peered down at the dead man, he now remembered seeing the markings at the crime scene. It had simply slipped his mind because so much had been going on.

"I also have somethin' else that may interest you," Wong said, blinking his eyes and turning to walk over to the x-ray machine.

He pointed at some x-rays taken of Prophet's body. "Look." Wong pointed with a stubby finger.

Agitated, Brown scratched his forehead. "I don't know how to read an x-ray."

"You no hafta read, look, see bullet," Wong said, raising his voice and jabbing his finger at the x-ray.

Brown leaned forward with his brow knotted, his eyes nar-rowed. In the rib cage area Brown saw what looked like tiny, luminous, star-shaped bullets.

"Bullets, the KTW Teflon armor-piercing Cop Killers," Brown muttered.

"Not just that," Wong added. "There another kind of bullet in the skull."

Brown raised his brow. "What kind?"

"I dunno, but we 'bout ta find out with eyetopsee," Wong said, blinking his eyes in intervals.

Barely five feet tall, Dr. Wong stood over Prophet as he carved the body with a scalpel. He swiftly cut a "T" incision, running the sharp blade from the shoulders to the sternum and down to the pelvic area, causing charred skin to peel away, exposing blood. The sound of flesh being cut was eerily slimy.

Dr. Wong then used a pair of shears as he hacked through the sternum. Vomit rose in the back of Brown's throat, causing him to grab his stomach and almost barf up all of the food he had eaten earlier.

"Hey! You no look so good. Why don't you go stand over by the garbage can. You no vomit on floor." Wong pointed with the bloody shears in his hand.

He then turned back around and stuck his hand inside the cavity of the body. The sound of his hand moving around inside the body cavity was gory. Brown winced and turned his head, placing his hand over his mouth. Wong removed a bullet and held it up to the light. Brown turned back around to face Dr. Wong. As he looked at the bullet, Brown's eyes watered as he struggled to keep his food down.

"What the fuck! The damn thing looks like an octopus," Brown said, looking at the bullet.

"It gets worse," Wong said, admiring the deadly bullet. "I found two different caliber bullets in the body."

"What?"

"The bullet that entered Prophet's cheek was from a .44," Wong said as he rinsed the bullet off in a weak solution of Clorox before bagging it.

"Why would someone want to use two different guns?" Brown asked out loud, perplexed.

There just seemed to be too many missing pieces to this puzzle. Wong went back over to the body with an electric saw and began to saw on Prophet's skull. That did it.

106

Brown couldn't take it anymore. He excused himself and headed for the exit door.

"You no wanna watch me do eyetopsee?" Wong yelled be-hind him.

The next morning Brown awakened in his small, but com-fortable, loft. Hauntingly, he remembered dreaming of dead bodies of beautiful women. It was Gina's face he saw in his dream...she chased him. He held his morning erection and thought about her as a yawn tugged at the corners of his mouth. The clock on the nightstand read 10:05 a.m. From his bedroom window a shy morning sun shined across his bed.

"Shit," he cursed as he sat up in the bed and reached for the phone.

He waited patiently as the operator put him on hold. Sud-denly, Rodriguez came on the line. He sounded winded. In the background, Brown heard the cacophony of loud voices in the police station. Instantly it hit him just how much he missed work.

"Detective Rodriguez, how may I help you?" Rodriguez asked.

"Rodriquez, it's me, Brown. Just calling to find out what's been going on with the Death Struck case."

Rodriguez lowered his voice to a conspiratorial tone. "Damn, Lieutenant, we miss the shit out 'cha 'round here." He looked around to see if anyone was listening to him and contin-ued, "I got some good news and some bad news."

Brown rolled his eyes on the other end of the phone as he planted his feet on the floor and cupped his head in his hands. "What?"

"The good news is, you remember the jewelry store robbery pictures of the woman with the blond wig?"

"Yeah."

"Well, Chief had the pictures sent to the FBI lab in Washington. The pictures are much better. You need to see them. We still don't have a make on the female, but these pictures gonna damn sho' help."

Rodriguez took the phone away from his ear. Brown could hear a struggle in the background. Someone was yelling, "Take your fucking hands off me!"

Rodriguez called out, "Don't fuckin' put 'em in the holding cell with the women. She's a he."

"Take your damn hands off me!" the voice repeated.

Rodriguez came back on the phone, "Shoo, fuckin' place is like a mad house. Okay, where was I?"

"The bad news."

"Oh yeah, the bad news. The feds are trying to take over the case, saying it's gang related—"

"That's bullshit!" Brown said, interrupting Rodriguez.

He stood and began to pace the floor in his boxer shorts. "Have you seen the morning news? The story about Damon Dice's body being discovered headless is the talk of the media. Captain Brooks was on CNN with the Mayor talking about a special task force being set up to investigate and arrest rappers."

"You know what I find so damn amazing? When a rapper gets killed they almost never find the killer, but when a rapper gets in trouble they can't wait to lock 'em up."

The two talked for a few more minutes. Before Brown hung up, Rodriguez agreed to keep him posted on anything that might be helpful about the case.

As he got dressed to begin his day, he thought about the new picture of the woman from the jewelry store robbery.

Twelve

Jack Lemon

Jack walked into the Tony building. Today he was conservatively dressed in a cream colored lambskin vest, white button-down cotton J. Lindeberg shirt, and black slacks with a pair of baby-soft Timberland boots. The diamond studs in his earlobes were as big as marbles. They were worth a fortune, but cost him nothing – thanks to Gina.

Today everything that he had ever done would come down to one moment – it was all or nothing. In a lot of ways he was entering the lion's den and he knew it. He had killed a man, forced his victim to watch, and afterward shot the victim in the ass after making him take part in the murder of his friend.

Jack was about to step to G-Solo, the new acting CEO and President of DieHard Records. This was a A Gangsta's Bitch move, especially if G-Solo had already flipped the script and went to them "folks." Jack could very well be walking into an ambush. Still, he had his trusty nine in his drawers. Jack had come for a takeover, just like the corporate gangsters do. The timing was just right, what with Damon's body popping up without a head.

That should have put the fear of God in them niggas, Jack thought. Now Jack was on some finesse time, just like the old heads in the joint had taught him. On this day Jack was feeling himself. He was in that element that only a thug can describe. Almost three months out the joint, young nigga on the grind, twenty-six years old stacking major paper. He had over two million in cash and jewelry stashed. Plus his man Rasheed had just got drafted to the pros. The thug god was definitely shining on a nigga, but somehow Jack's mind drifted back to the white bitch Georgia Mae. One thing he had to admit, she gave some smoking head and ass. He wondered if she'd tricked Rasheed too with that fat ass of hers. One thing for sure, if she stayed around too long, Monique was in serious trouble.

Jack refocused his mind back on the matter at hand. His mind chimed like a song. "It's better to be feared than loved," Jack said over and over again.

Finesse was a wise man's game, understood by a limited few, used by even less. The press move was dangerous. Too much pressure could burst an iron pipe and often the only way to find out if the press had backfired was if the vic went to the police.

As Jack walked on, he ignored the opulent wealth of the building as well as some of the white faces that looked at him. Earlier that day, he had called, pretending to be a reporter checking to see if G-Solo would be in his office. He was informed that he would be in the office giving interviews until two o'clock.

Up ahead, Jack saw the security guard sitting at a booth. He was looking at a newspaper. Occasionally the guard would look up as he checked people's names off some sort of list before he gave them access to the elevator located behind him.

"Shit," Jack cursed under his breath as his pace slowed.

People continued to walk all around him with the hum of a busy work day. As Jack spied the elevator, he saw an attractive woman step out. She had a caramel complexion with a generous figure. Standing behind her was the biggest, blackest man that Jack had ever seen in his entire life. She strode by, giving Jack a quick once over. He watched her ass wave from side to side.

"Bootylicious fo-reel, huh," Jack said out the side of his mouth, making her giggle girlishly as she strutted by.

Her bodyguard grilled Jack with the screw face as he walked by, making it his business to brush into him. Jack found himself once again refocusing back to the matter at hand – how to get past the security guard.

Casually Jack walked over to the directory and scanned the names. DieHard Records was on the twenty-sixth floor. Jack heard the elevator door ding open. People stepped out. A fat woman with a briefcase on wheels walked over and said something to the security guard, causing him to turn his head. Jack made a beeline straight for the elevator. Now was the hard part – boldly walking into enemy territory. It was all or nothing. He pushed the button.

The elevator went up, making his heart flutter as soft classical music piped through speakers. At the twenty-sixth floor, the door chimed open. Jack was instantly confronted by a mob of niggas. He reached for his strap.

Someone in the crowd yelled, "Yo, son! Dat's my nigga! Dat's my nigga!"

Jack stood back and scanned the crowd, a sea of mean mug faces. His mind frantically tried to decide friend or foe before he pulled out his burner. A dark-skinned, well-built man shoved his way through the crowd of what looked like a crew of over fifty people whose loyalty to him was written in the scowls on their faces.

Keyvon Jackson, better known to those around him as 40 smiled brightly, like a five hundred watt bulb. His smile was infectious as he walked up and bear hugged Jack.

"Nigga, wuz really good?" 40 said joyously as he firmly held Jack's shoulder with his hand.

Jack fell back and kept his emotions in check, conscious that niggas had 40 on some celebrity type shit. True, he was that, but Jack knew the nigga back in the day when he was Keyvon and they was both flat feet hustling. It was important that 40 didn't get shit twisted. Jack was Jack, the same nigga he used to smoke trees with. It didn't take long for 40 to detect Jack's aloofness.

As they stepped back inside the elevator, his crew tried to follow. "Hold up," 40 said, throwing up his hand, the diamond and platinum bracelet sparkling like blue and white fire. "Let me holla at dis nigga for a sec. Me and dude go way back." As 40 spoke, the smile on his face dimmed like he was trying to read Jack's thoughts while the doors to the elevator closed.

He pushed the button to make the car stop. He wanted to talk to his longtime friend.

"Nigga, when you come home? Tell me what you need … anything. I got the whole industry on lock." 40 was hyper, talking a mile a minute.

However, he was conscious of the void, the huge gap that stood between them. Maybe it was just time, two friends being away from each other for too long. One thing 40 seemed to know for certain, Jack Lemon wasn't your average nigga. 40 had not sent Jack a dime while he was away. It was nothing intentional, shit was just moving too fast.

"Son, I'm tellin' ya, I got this bitch on blast. I'm the dopest rapper eva!" 40 bragged.

Jack looked at him and cocked his head to the side as if he wasn't impressed. "Yeah, Keyvon, you nice, got the game on lock, don't 'cha," Jack chided.

40 could sense the insincerity in Jack's statement. The mo-ment suddenly became awkward as classical music played in the background. Keyvon shrugged his shoulders, as if to throw the façade of "entertainer" away, so that he could come with the realness.

His voice lowered a pitch as he pushed his lips forward with purposeful intent. "What da fuck is going on with you, nigga? I still got mad love for ya." Jack turned to face him, his mind searching for the right words. Keyvon exhaled deeply and continued, "You think a nigga done changed, huh? Well, let me tell you something. A nigga that say money don't change you is telling a damn lie, but I ain't never, never gonna forget where I come from. Word! When a nigga hit me up eight times you was da first muthafucka at my hospital bed." He pounded his fist hard inside the palm of his hand. "Hell, when I was on my dick, you gave a nigga his first work." He thought for a moment then started laughing as his eyes stayed on Jack. "We played hooky from school, use ta twist out bitches together. I remember the time with big booty Brenda. You pulled out the jammy and killed the poonaney. Horse-dick-ass nigga. By the time I went, it was like a truck had just drove through her." Keyvon laughed some more. Jack couldn't help but smile.

Keyvon looked at his watch, chuckled and then turned se-rious again. "Yo, B, you need anything, car, clothes, cash, or hoes, holla at 'cha boy. "

"Yo, I'm good, son," Jack said, turning to face Keyvon, looking him in his eyes with an ice cold stare. "I got a problem, but money ain't one of them."

"Nigga, just tell me what you want, what your problem is."

Jack raised his voice as he cut his eyes into optic slants. "Nigga, you da problem!"

"What?" Keyvon frowned as his jaw dropped.

"Nigga, believe it or not, you the dopest rapper since Tupac and Biggie, but you're playin' right into these crackas' hands with all this beef shit you keep kickin' up with the home team."

"Nigga, what you talkin' 'bout? Big Dolla 'n dem niggas?" 40 said with a frown like he couldn't believe Jack was going to side with them, too.

"Word, son, I'm feelin' you, but that's why the East Coast, West Coast rivalry shit was invented in the first place, so they could make it look like black men killin' each other when in reality it's them crackas who got a hand in most of the killins. Like throwing a rock and hiding the hand. The bad part is, they gonna kill you, too."

"Whaaat?!" Keyvon gasped, looking at Jack like he had lost his fuckin' mind.

Jack softened his voice to almost a plea. "Yo, you a young nigga, both of us is, but it's power. Money is power. Hip-hop is power and the mic is powerful – powerful enough to affect an entire election, to change laws. Like it or not, you're the next emperor to the throne of hip-hop.

Nigga, you gotta humble yourself. You can either bring us closer together or separate us further apart. Just think if we ran hip-hop like white folks run corporate America or Wall Street. A nigga ain't gonna get one of them ten-million-dollar-a-year jobs. They ain't gonna let a nigga make that kind of money cause they know how to play they position.

"White folks could be enemies and still find a way to come together to fuck us up, and then go back to being enemies. Regardless of they beef, when it comes to breakin' bread with each other they gonna bond like fuckin' glue to make sure we don't get nothin' but fuckin' crumbs." As Jack spoke, 40 nodded his head like he was starting to get the point, then someone began banging on the elevator door.

Jack lowered his voice, "My nigga, I'm tellin' ya what God love, the truth. A lot of niggas fitna come up missing, crackas too. Label executives, owners and just about everybody that got they hand in this shit and not helpin' our people."

Suddenly Keyvon's eyes shot wide open. "Damon Dice's body was found with his dome missing."

"Yep, it's gonna be a lot mo' just like that, na'mean," Jack said with a straight face.

Keyvon nodded. "I never liked the nigga no way ... and I feel what you tryna do, bring all the good cats together to take over the industry on a business level." He leaned up against the wood grain of the elevator, placing his foot up against the wall and pondered everything Jack had just said. With a deep breath, he began to speak. "Word, I'll find a way to place all my differences aside, let shit ride. Yo, I got a seed on the way," Keyvon said, thinking to the present.

"This shit ain't all glamour. I miss dem days Jack, when a nigga used to be able to run carefree and wild."

Jack looked at his old friend, the bullet-proof vest, the ar-mored cars and the fifty-man crew waiting for him on the other side of the elevator doors. Keyvon Jackson now lived within the fortress that his persona had built. He was trying to survive, to stay sucker free.

"Yo, where the fuck you get dem stones you got in your ears?" 40 asked, admiring Jack's diamonds as he pushed the button for the elevator door to open—his way of discreetly changing the subject and getting back into character.

As the door opened Jack said, "I might be working on a project soon. Might need your help. A nigga got a mil in the stash, wuz up?"

"That's enough for about five tracks," 40 bragged.

"Get the fuck outta here," Jack said, punching him in the shoulder.

"Nigga, you betta ask somebody. You been gone too long, shit poppin'!" 40 extended his hand. "You fam, just make it happen and I'll work with ya." They hugged as 40's crew looked on.

Afterward, they exchanged digits and Jack bounced down the hall to the next phase. Jack walked a short distance and came to a lobby and turned the corner. He was confronted by a cute secretary with short stylish hair, a pecan complexion and an pleasant oval face. She looked to be no older than eighteen with her small perky breasts and long golden acrylic fingernails accentuated with gold rings on each finger. She sat behind the handsome, large, oak desk, clearly fascinated with something on her computer screen. Jack spied the name on the door to her right, DieHard Records.

As he approached, he cleared his throat, startling the woman and causing her to look up. Her wide ebony eyes were the most beautiful shade of brown that Jack had ever seen, a teenage version of Toni Braxton. She pushed the ESC button on the computer, but not before Jack saw the porn she was looking at – two people having sex on the floor doggy style. With her crooked smile, she looked up as she held a wad of blue bubble gum in the corner of her mouth.

"I'm Mr. Baker from downstairs on the seventeenth floor. There's a package at the elevator for DieHard, that you?" Jack asked, pleased to watch the girl spring to her feet as her perky titties jiggled.

She excused herself, pulled at her tight skirt and awkwardly walked by him in her high heels. Her little tooty booty, barely a handful, stuck out conspicuously. As soon as she turned the corner of the hallway, Jack adjusted his pants and walked through the door to DieHard Records. G-Solo was in for a big surprise.

Stealthily Jack closed the door behind him. The inside of the office was decorated like a palace with expensive crystal and plush carpeting. The walls were adorned with gold and platinum records. A large, bigger-than-life picture window overlooked the city.

Damn! Jack thought to himself once again. These niggas livin' large. Jack crinkled his nose as he smelled the sweet aroma of weed. He noticed a gray haze of smoke drifting toward the window like a miniature cloud.

He then heard the indistinguishable sound of slurping and sucking. It segued into lustful drones of "Ahhh, mmm, ohhh …that's it. That's it. Go faster, suck it, girl."

It took only a second for Jack to recognize the passionate moans and groans. The sounds were coming from behind an impressive ivory and black marble wrought-iron desk with a matching La-Z-Boy loveseat. The chair was facing the opposite direction from Jack. He continued to creep forward, unbutton-ing his vest for easy access to his strap.

"Emm, errr …" Jack cleared his throat.

The chair quickly swiveled around to face Jack. G-Solo was nude except for the platinum chain around his neck and the diamond bracelets on his wrist. He had a smoldering blunt in his hand and one of the baddest chicks Jack had ever seen bent down, ass up, with his dick in her mouth.

She stood up so fast, her conical breasts bounced like springboards. Her skin appeared flawless and was the color of maple syrup. There was a slight sheen of perspiration on her that glistened in the sunlight coming through the window. She had a slight Bugs Bunny overbite that gave her that ghetto fabulous sex appeal. With one had on her wide hip and the other over her mouth, she giddily blurted out a giggle. Her pop bottle figure was audaciously curved. The small bush between her legs was trimmed and shaped like a heart. She had a gap between her legs big enough to stick a fist through.

"Nigga, what da fuck you doin' in here?" G-Solo yelled through clinched teeth. He spoke as if they were superglued. Thanks to Jack's earlier handiwork, his jaw was wired shut.

"Calm the fuck down," Jack said, gesturing with his hand up like a cop stopping traffic.

"Fuck you mean, nigga? I'm calling the police." G-Solo reached for the phone.

Jack was now faced with his worst nightmare. This nigga was getting ready to make a bogus move and force Jack to wet him and the chick up. Jack's mind churned up old lessons learned in a cell, as his fingers instinctively inched toward his burner.

Better to be feared than loved, he remembered.

"Hello, I need the police here—"

"I'm a friend of a friend. They sent me," Jack said evenly, with his hand under his vest. He was less than a second from killing G-Solo and the chick.

Instantly, G-Solo froze.

Oh shit, he thought to himself. A friend of a friend. He knew what that meant. He thought back to the night Big Prophet was killed and what the gunman had told him. With Damon Dice's body recently discovered, minus a head, it didn't take a rocket scientist to know these "friends," whoever they were, were not playing games. Fear gripped G-Solo's body like a gigantic hand. He slammed the phone down like he had received an electrical shock.

"Oh shit, goddamn," G-Solo muttered, as the image of him pulling the trigger and shooting his man Prophet in the face on that dark and gloomy night flashed through his mind.

The whole time, the chick looked back and forth between the two men with her finger pressed against her chin, leaning to one side.

She muttered as if talking to herself, "He's kinda cute."

G-Solo looked up at her annoyed. The broad was dingy as hell. "Baby, get yo' shit and get outta here." She made a face, filling her rosy cheeks with air and expelling it as she folded her arms over her breasts. It suddenly occurred to Jack just who the chick looked like – Melyssa Ford, the broad that did all the videos. Jack admired her nude body.

The door suddenly burst open and in walked the young sec-retary that Jack had earlier eluded. "You!" She pointed, still holding that wad of gum in her mouth. "The police are on their way."

"No! No! No!" G-Solo screamed as he jumped to his feet, penis swinging.

The secretary took one look at the scene and her mouth flew open. The Melyssa Ford chick snickered at the secretary. The young girl had covered her eyes and was peeking through her fingers.

"I … I … I got everything under control. We don't need the police," G-Solo stuttered.

"But, you called security," the flustered secretar y wailed.

"Leave!" G-Solo said as he pointed at the door.

The secretary's shoulders slumped as she backtracked her steps, mumbling something about telling mama.

"You tell mama and your ass will be working at Chuck E. Cheese again!" G-Solo yelled behind her.

He then cursed as he slung the blunt that he had still been holding at the desk after it burned his hand.

"Girl, put your clothes on. You gotta go," he said with a frown, his eyes focusing on Jack.

G-Solo reached down and picked up a bundle of clothes and handed them to the woman. Jack did a double take, thinking about all the times in the joint he used to jack his dick on the XXL magazines with the sexy pictorials of the real Melyssa Ford, leaving his fingers sticky. Now as he watched her look-alike bent over, ass jiggling from side to side as she squeezed into a thong, he thought of all the things he could do to her that would make her sticky.

Jack forced his mind to other matters as he made an assess-ment of the situation – the dangers, the risks, the advantages and the disadvantages. One thing was certain, G-Solo sure in the hell wasn't mourning the death of his man Damon Dice. He was sitting in Dice's office smoking weed, getting his dick sucked by a broad that was a dime piece. In fact, it looked like the skinny nigga was celebrating Damon's death. Jack reached back into his mind and retrieved all the information he had forced out of Damon.

The broad continued to smile and flirt with Jack with her eyes as she was putting her clothes on. She licked the rim of her lips, showing off her tongue ring, a seductive dick tease.

On her way out the door she caroled, "Haaaay G, call me tonight. If you like, bring a friend." She gave Jack her best "I wanna fuck you" eyes and strutted out the door.

G-Solo turned to face Jack, his eyes searching. The eleven false teeth inserted into G-Solo's mouth made him resemble a beaver and the wired braces made it almost impossible for him to open his mouth.

"Have a seat," Jack said as the two men stood considering each other.

G-Solo frowned and pulled up his pants. "Friend of a friend … you killed Prophet?"

"No, he killed his muthafuckin' self doin' that dumb shit by talking slick out the mouth, selling death and conspiring with snitches. Dude was executed and you helped pull the trigger." Jack pointed at himself. "I had nothing to do with it."

"They made me pull the trigger," G-Solo said, breathing hard, face stricken with misery regarding what he had done. " Where's the gun?" G-Solo asked with more courage than he was actually feeling.

The blunt that G-Solo had flung on the desk just moments earlier caught Jack's attention. It was still burning, now with a long ash. Jack felt like he was having withdrawal. He wanted to hit it so bad that he could taste it, but since the episode with Georgia Mae, he was cool. You can learn a lot from a white woman.

Jack's mind went straight to press game mode. It's better to be feared than loved.

Finesse was the key to manipulation in the press game. "I came to save your life," he said reassuringly, ignoring his question. "I'm your friend. I love your music. I was sent here to help you, but you're gonna have to keep it real with me. These people are cold-blooded killers," Jack said, running his press game.

"You came to help me?" G-Solo whined with his teeth wired shut. "Then help me get that gun back, pahleez man. If that gun gets into the wrong hands with my prints on it, I could get in big trouble."

"Yeah, I know," Jack said, feigning sympathy as he nodded his head. "You could also end up in the electric chair, but if you're lucky they'll just give you a couple of life sentences."

"Ohhh, nooo, you gotta help me!" G-Solo drawled with a frown on his face like he was about to cry. He was a big ball of nerves.

"Nigga, didn't I tell ya that's what I'm here for?" Jack said, asserting himself.

It was just like being a war daddy to one of them soft-ass niggas in the joint. As long as they felt you were going to protect them, the money kept coming.

"It really ain't all that bad. You're now overseeing DieHard's daily functions." G-Solo shot Jack a glare like he was crazy. "You seen this morning's news? Damon's body was found…" he paused for a second and said, "headless." G-Solo made a face.

Jack slowly took a few steps then stood a few feet away from him. "You really don't seem to be too concerned about it. Your man's missing his wig, dead as a muhfuh, and you in here smokin' and getting your dick sucked by that video bitch."

Lost for words, G-Solo moved his lips, but no words es-caped.

"Listen nigga, with Damon out the way all this is now yours," Jack said, spreading his arms. "The people that sent me got a master plan. Part of the plan is to make you rich beyond your wildest dreams." With that said, G-Solo leaned forward. Jack had his attention. "However, these people in high places, they also wouldn't mind seeing you and Phyllis dead." G-Solo's head snapped back like he had just received an upper cut and his eyes stretched damn near out the sockets.

"Phyllis, how my ole girl get into this?"

"Nigga, you know the rules. Your mama gotta go, too. These cats that sent me, they don't play!"

With tears in his eyes, G-Solo asked what Jack wanted him to do. Jack asked for the location of the financial records for DieHard's earnings.

"I'll hafta ask my sister, I mean my secretary, to get all the information off the computer." G-Solo grimaced and wiped his nose with the back of his hand.

The two stood and looked at each other, neither saying a word. Jack looked at the phone on the desk then back at G-Solo. He knew what that meant. He picked up the phone and told his secretary to gather all of the company's financial information and bring it to him.

After hanging up the phone, he looked at the clock and be-gan speaking. "I'm scheduled to have a meeting in a few minutes with the head of Tony Records, Michael Cobin. DieHard's contract expires this week. We're behind schedule with the albums of the other four groups on the label and Mr. Cobin is pressuring me to find a new CEO and President."

"Have you found anybody?"

"Nope, and I don't know what to do. I'm scared, man. I'm only twenty years old." G-Solo's voice cracked and his eyes slid to the floor as he looked at Jack for help.

"Tell you what," Jack said, taking a seat across from G-Solo. "Every man got a mission, a purpose in life. Know what I mean. You make music; I make men, like iron sharpens steel. I was born into this shit. I'm the son of a revolutionary, so I was born ta die. I'ma take you unda' my wing," Jack said, spitting game like flavor in your ear as he stared at the frightened man-child sitting across from him.

For the first time, G-Solo's face brightened up. A glint of hope shined in his eyes as he bobbed his head up and down.

"Together, you and I fitna put this rap game on lock, make it so we can open doors for mo' cats that's hungry. I'ma teach 'cha how to think big. Now, I know you wonderin' if a nigga preachin' this black man conscious shit, why I'm rollin' wit' a team of killas? Simple, these sell-out niggas like some fuckin' disease, like cancer. They snitchin' and workin' against our people to help the man. Son, these niggas have to be dealt with. Black folks made twelve billion dollars last year. We gave ninety-five percent of it away. We think we pimpin', but we gettin' pimped by the system. White folks, Asians, Arabs and Indians got liquor stores, beauty supply shops, gas stations and shit in our hood, and they don't spend one fuckin' dime with us. They keep one hundred percent of their wealth in their communities to send their children to the best schools, to uplift their culture, fo-reel, fo-reel, they don't give a fuck 'bout us," Jack said with so much emotion that he grimaced in a hateful scowl.

"Nigga, you gotta have love fo' your people if you gonna roll with me," Jack said as the secretary sashayed across the carpet with her tooty booty wagging.

She rolled her eyes at Jack, causing him to laugh dryly. She then placed the information he had asked for on the desk and walked back out the door.

Jack picked it up and thumbed through the reports hungrily. It listed various categories: Annual earnings, Budgets, Revenues. Revenues?

Jack scanned the section detailing DieHard's revenues. The combined earnings overseas and in the United States came to a total of forty-seven million dollars. Jack whistled through his teeth. He was impressed with last year's earnings.

Then he frowned as he looked up from the paper. "You only made five hundred grand this year?" he asked G-Solo.

"Yep, and I still owe Mr. Cobin eighty G's."

"How's dat?" Jack asked.

"I have to pay for the limo, security and some other bills."

Jack shook his head, something wasn't right.

"Where's yo' lawyer?"

"What lawyer? We use Mr. Cobin's lawyer. His name is Da-vid Steel. I trust him."

Hearing that, Jack tossed the papers into the air. He was livid. What was with this nigga, G-Solo? Was he that stupid?

"Never trust a cracka, period! You wanna know why?"

G-Solo shrugged his shoulders. "Why?"

"Crackas don't trust each other, so you know damn well that after all that hideous shit they do to niggas they don't really expect us to trust them, and when they find one of them turn- the-otha-cheek-ass niggas, they teach him a lesson, too. Just like Cobin is doin' you," Jack said, barely able to contain himself. Jack thought for a second with his fingers interlocked under his chin. "I'm going to that meeting with you. You gonna tell Cobin I'm your choice for the new CEO of DieHard."

"But, you don't have no experience."

"Nigga, don't worry 'bout that. I got more than you. Besides, I got a feelin' this Cobin dude would rather have two dumb niggas in charge than one."

"But he's gonna want to know 'bout your past."

"Don't worry 'bout dat. Just have the papers drawn up with me on salary. Where is the meeting s'pose ta be?" Jack asked eagerly.

"Down the hall," G-Solo replied dubiously, like he wasn't feeling the plan.

Jack spent the remaining minutes schooling G-Solo on what to say to the white man, Mr. Cobin. G-Solo attended the meeting with Jack by his side. G-Solo was shaking like crooked dice in a crap game full of killers. Jack played his position, stayed on the sidelines, low key. The office was spacious, with plaques and lots of pictures of rappers on the walls.

Mr. Cobin had a long hatchet face, narrow shoulders and a slim, willowy build. His blue eyes seemed to always be watchfully alert— like a man who was sure of himself. They were all seated around his desk. Another man was in the room, David Steel, one of Tony's attorneys. He specialized in record contracts. He wore a perpetual smirk along with a pencil thin mustache. He was dressed in a three-thousand-dollar pinstriped suit.

So, this is corporate AmeriKKKa, home of the real gang-sters, Jack thought to himself as he soaked up the scene. Mr. Cobin and his henchmen lawyer whispered to each other from time to time. Jack swore he could read their minds. Something about the two white men just wasn't right. Cobin started off with some drawn out act about his condolences for his dead friend Damon Dice. He then went on to talk about how the music industr y was going to surely miss him.

Finally, Cobin cut his eyes at Jack as he inquired about him and, just as they rehearsed, G-Solo went over the spiel about Jack being the man to take over Damon Dice's position as CEO and President of DieHard Records. Cobin grinned slyly. He had worked with urban blacks since rappers Run DMC came on the scene in the 80s, so he knew it wasn't nothing unusual for an ex-felon or street hustler to take over a hip-hop record label and make it successful.

One thing that Cobin did find interesting about Jack Lemon was that he exuded an air of confidence that you didn't see in most young black men. It didn't really matter, though. By the time his lawyers got finished manipulating the figures, most of the artists in the business were lucky to break even. G-Solo was one of them.

If he picked a CEO for DieHard Records, the man had to be just as dumb as he was, Cobin figured, as he looked at Jack with a smirk. For the first time, Jack wished he had a lawyer as he listened to the terms of DieHard's new contract agreement. G-Solo would be given a million dollar signing bonus and each one of the artists on the label who renewed their contracts would receive five hundred thousand. The contract had all kinds of incentives. If G-Solo sold over five million copies of his CD, they would give him five dollars of each sale, plus he could renegotiate the terms of the entire contract, with the right to buy it out at the cost that Tony had originally paid for it.

However, if G-Solo failed to meet the terms of his contract, he would only be given sixty cents of each record and his bonus would be reduced to four hundred thousand dollars. The million dollar signing bonus would become null and void, meaning he would be forced to pay back all additional monies. The same would apply to each artist on the DieHard label.

"I'm not signing that!" G-Solo huffed, barely understandable through all of the wire in his mouth.

"You stand to gain just over seventy-five million if you can complete the terms. Your last CD sold over two million. I have faith in you. I think it's a good contract with a good artist," Michael Cobin said as he glanced over at the lawyer for approval.

The lawyer nodded like a puppet.

"I'm still in doubt from the last album. If I fail I'll be even more in debt with you," G-Solo complained in a whiny voice that irritated Jack.

"That's even more reason to sign the contract – to get out of debt," Cobin said.

Jack was all eyes and ears. Cobin was convincing and slick just like any hustler on the Brooklyn streets, only Cobin wore a suit and tie. Jack reached over and took the contract out of G-Solo's hand. The two white men watched him closely, the way a fox watches the chickens.

Jack took a deep breath and looked up from the paper. In the pit of his gut he knew he should have had a lawyer going over the documents with him. "So, basically, that you're saying is, if our sales are over five million dollars,

DieHard Records will receive five dollars of each sale, plus we'll be able to buy back our contract if we decide to take an offer from another record label?"

"Exactly," Michael Cobin said, smiling for the first time as he folded his arms on the desk. "However, as I stated earlier, if you fail to meet the terms of the contract, there is a forfeit clause in the contract. Did I mention that?" Cobin shrugged his shoulders and chuckled. "If you fail to meet the terms of this very gracious contract, DieHard Records will become the sole possession of Tony Records. That is, until you can repay the defaulted monies back at nineteen percent interest."

"We'll lose the company if we don't sell the records?" Jack asked.

"The company, the artists, the rights to use the name and all royalties." As Cobin listed all the things they could lose, G-Solo noticeably cringed.

"We stand to gain over seventy-five million?" Jack asked.

"Yes, and more if you go on tour and sales go well. The last album did extremely well overseas."

"Sign it," Jack said, never taking his eyes off Cobin.

"No, I'm not signing that!" G-Solo screeched.

"Sign it now!" Jack raised his voice.

Hesitantly, G-Solo signed the document with a gold pen that Cobin's lawyer had shoved in his face. Cobin looked on, pleased.

After G-Solo signed the contract, the lawyer quickly snatched it up.

"Glad to have you on board," Cobin said, extending his hand to Jack. "I love a man with balls and integrity, not afraid to take a chance." Jack shook his hand firmly and kept his thoughts to himself.

Cobin might as well have been telling him to bend over; he was about to fuck Jack with Vaseline. Afterward Jack was given an office down the hall from G-Solo's, as well as a salar y based on the sales of the DieHard records. Jack let it be known that he would be bringing a team of lawyers, accountants, advisors and others to work with the artists as well. Cobin gave him a look of good riddance.

Jack paced the floor with his hand cupped under his chin. They were back in G-Solo's office. The phone had been ringing like crazy. G-Solo's limo driver was waiting downstairs along with a bodyguard that had shown up late for work again.

G-Solo fired up the blunt on his desk. He was a nervous wreck. Jack stopped pacing and glanced over at him. The kid was barely twenty years old, and just like all the other rap artists before him who had been given their own independent record labels, and in most cases didn't have a clue about the business aspect of it, G-Solo spent most of his days hanging out at the mall signing autographs with his boys and hitting on chicks. If he wasn't doing that, he spent his time stunting around in the extra stretch Maybach limousine, fucking bitches and getting blowed.

As Jack looked at his baby face, G-Solo blew a thick cloud of smoke up at the ceiling. Jack's urge to hit the blunt was so bad he felt like a junkie in withdrawal.

"Yo, son, from this point on we gonna stack some chips and stop making white folks rich off us. Just like how Master P. did," Jack said as he watched G-Solo pull deeply on the blunt and make a face before choking on the smoke.

The phone rang again.

"Call me back later," G-Solo spoke into the receiver and hung up.

"I'm tellin' ya now, your whole crew, everybody from body-guards to publicists are being fired. I'm bringing in a whole new DieHard team. This cracka, Cobin, he thinks that we just some dumb-ass niggas," Jack said as he walked over to the window with its majestic view of New York City, where down below, people looked like ants.

"I'm callin' in the big guns. The shit gonna be big. You're gonna work wit' Big Dolla and 40."

"That ain't gonna happen. Them niggas don't get along with each other," G-Solo confirmed.

Jack spun around from the window. "Can't you see, that's the beauty of it all? These niggas the home team. They the heart and soul of hip-hop. The trick is to bring them together." Jack's voice was filled with emotion as he spoke about a facet of his dream.

"One thing I learned about us human beings is that every-body got a price," Jack said.

"Man, I don't know."

"Just do what the fuck I tell ya. I'm investing a mil of my own money on this project. You just hope that we can pull it off, 'cause if not, your ass hit, son."

"Hit? It wasn't my idea to sign that contract."

Jack had to exercise patience with him and not lose sight of using finesse with the kid. With a calm voice he spoke, "You're in a lot of trouble with the gun and all. I'm tr yna to help you, but right now you need to focus all your attention on what you do best, which is writing rhymes and setting up studio time for long hours. I intend to have all the projects on this label finished within the next two months. In the meantime, I'm getting in contact with all the gym shoe corporations to ink us a deal, and we're going to get started on a line of DieHard clothing. Hopefully, we can do a soundtrack for a movie or two. Get ready, you're going to be working with 40's camp."

With that said, Jack headed for the door. He knew it sounded good, but could it work? It had to. Jack was a hustler.

Within days Jack's new agent had inked a deal in a brilliant move with a woman by the name of Traycee Pagan. She had turned one of her bestselling books, Life, into a motion picture, with an unheard of budget for an urban film – seventy-five million. Several big-name stars were to act in the movie. Michael Cobin would be in for a big surprise in the coming months.

Thirteen

Rasheed & Georgia Mae

Two months after Rasheed was drafted and had signed a deal with the New York Knicks, in a pre-season game for the NBA rookies, he was leading scorer. In that same game, he went up for a dunk and came down wrong on his leg, shattering his knee. The bone popped so loud that some said they could hear it all the way up in the top of the stands. Rasheed was rushed to the emergency room. The dunk was captured on film and ESPN's SportsCenter replayed the footage of Rasheed's injury over and over again every thirty minutes.

When Monique got the call all the way in California where she was modeling, she bugged out. Later she watched the replay on SportsCenter and cried again. No human being's legs were supposed to bend back that far. She wanted to fly home immediately, but she was scheduled to fly to Paris for her first big shoot for "Gentlemen's Magazine." Plus, they were paying her ten thousand dollars a day. She was scheduled to stay for a week and a half, then she would be shooting in Brazil.

Everything had been going well for Monique. Not only did she get the job as a model for the illustrious "Gentlemen's Magazine", but she also earned a position as centerfold in the magazine and sales for that month were at an all-time high.

She called Rasheed from her hotel room. Monique was al-ready packed and ready to catch her flight with the rest of the girls on a private jet, courtesy of the founder and owner of Gentlemen's Enterprises.

Rasheed answered on the fourth ring. He sounded winded.

"Hello."

"Ra, are you alright? I saw what happened on television—"

"It's torn up pretty bad. When are you coming home?"

"I … I'm going to try to get there as soon as I get back from Paris."

"Paris? Mo, baby, I'm having second thoughts about you taking that job. We hardly ever see each other, and oh, some of the fellas on the team have seen your photo spread in the magazine."

Silence.

"Listen, baby," Monique said with a small voice. "This is my first assignment. Out of thirty-eight women I am the only sista. These people have paid me a lot of money. For me to back out now could hurt my career."

"Your career?" Rasheed raised his voice. "What about my fuckin' leg, what about me and the baby?"

"Ra, I'm sorr y. I hoped that you could understand. I prom-ise to make it back as soon as this is over with."

She could hear him breathing on the phone. What she had to say next she knew would sound as if she were more concerned about their finances than him, but she had to ask, it was important.

"Ra, baby, did you sign the insurance policy like I asked you to?" She could hear him sigh audibly as he muttered something under his breath.

"Uhh, hmm, next year I'm renewing my contract ... baby, when you comin' home?" Rasheed said, sounding disgruntled as he skirted around her question.

"So you didn't sign the policy," Monique said with grit in her voice.

Rasheed writhed in pain as he sat on the couch in the plush confines of the condo he had just purchased. He shifted uncomfortably. The cast on his leg was all the way from his ankle to his upper thigh. Doctors had installed four rods. He would need several more surgeries just to be able to walk normally again.

"I need you," he spoke into the receiver, not answering her question. He shifted as he spoke. "Mo ... I'll put the key under the mat on the front. Baby, please come back tonight. They don't need you. I do."

Monique's heart broke at the sound of his plea, but he still hadn't answered her question. "What about the insurance policy, Rasheed?" she spoke with more force in her voice.

"How can you even think of an insurance policy at a time like this? Damnit, Mo, everything is 'bout fuckin' money with you now, just because you make about as much as me."

"No, it's just that the new house you bought Grandma Hat-tie and all the cars and the condo, everything is in your name and ..."

Monique couldn't finish her statement. She hated when he made her feel guilty. He had turned the tables like it was all her fault, like she didn't care. So, in the end they both avoided acknowledging the possibility of Rasheed not being able to ever play again.

The rest of their conversation, all two minutes of it, was a strained dialogue. He hung up without saying goodbye. After-ward, Monique cried and convinced herself that maybe she was overreacting.

One thing was certain – she needed to get back home as soon as possible to cater to her man. Then she had an idea. Still sniffling, she picked up the phone and called her girl Georgia Mae. They had become best friends. Sympathetically, Georgia Mae assured Monique that everything would be okay. The two friends chatted for hours. Before hanging up the phone, Georgia Mae assured Monique that she'd go by and check on Rasheed. That's what real girlfriends are for. Right?

It wasn't two hours after Georgia Mae got off of the phone with Monique that she showed up at Rasheed's condo dressed provocatively. She wore a skin-tight, fire-red sequined mini dress that revealed lots of cleavage. When she moved, her butt shook like drug store jelly. Georgia Mae was a woman on a mission. NBA players weren't plentiful these days. She pushed up her bosom and rapped on the door.

Moments later, Rasheed appeared, looking haggard and weary. He was teetering on crutches. Georgia Mae gasped like she was in total shock.

"Forgive me, but I had to come by and check on you and Monique. I heard about your injury on the news. Rasheed, I'm so sorry," Game said on the verge of tears.

Something about her kindness deeply touched him as he answered, "Monique isn't here."

"Nooo," Georgia Mae animatedly droned as she laced her hand over her mouth, shaking her head somberly. "I can't believe Monique isn't here for you at a time like this. You need somebody to look after you," Georgia Mae said as she walked through the door.

"She's in California 'bout to fly to Paris for some damn pho-to shoot," Rasheed spat bitterly as he watched Georgia Mae strut by, her eyes roaming over the handsome décor of the condo.

Rasheed had hired an interior decorator to set his place up. Georgia Mae spun on her heels as Rasheed limped toward her.

"Poor baby," she cooed like a sex kitten, lips pushed forward like she was about to give him a sultry, wet kiss. With her chest pushed forward she said, "Monique is wrong! She needs to be here for you."

Rasheed dropped his head. "You're right. I was thinking the same thing. It's like, all she thinks about is money now-a-days."

"Humph, they say money is the true test of a relationship, makes people change."

He nodded his head in agreement and sat down on the couch.

Georgia Mae sat down next to him, placing her hand on his thigh, fingers twirling.

"I still can't believe Monique would choose her career over you. This just ain't right," she said as if she were really upset with Monique. Her hand stalled on Rasheed's lap, making tiny circles.

"You look like you're in pain. Did they give you any pain medicine?" she asked.

"Yeah." He threw his head back on the couch and closed his eyes as her fingers crawled closer. "They gave me some shit, but it's not working all that well," he said, sighing.

"I got somethin' betta fo' ya," Georgia Mae said in a husky voice dripping with seduction.

She inched closer, her nipple brushing against his chest. She unzipped his pants, but Rasheed opened his eyes and grabbed her hand.

"Go ahead, stop me. Stop me from doing all the things that Monique should be here doing, loving you and taking care of you," Georgia Mae said as she slowly got down on her knees.

He just looked at her with a raised brow as she moved his hand, and with her teeth unzipped his fly, her lipstick staining his pants. His enormous erection was throbbing as she pulled his penis out. She licked her lips and slowly she licked the head around the rim like it was a delicious tootsie pop, all the while her eyes watched him. He grabbed hold of the couch cushion as she placed the head in her mouth, slowly taking him in. He was thick, long and large. She would have to use both hands and all the muscles in her mouth.

He palmed the back of her head, aiding her mouth to take him deeper, and to his surprise, she did. She went much deeper as she found a rhythm. She hummed with his dick in her mouth. That seemed to excite him more, the way she made her mouth vibrate as her long tongue salivated, licking, sucking and playing with his balls. She made him arch his back off the couch to meet her deep in the back of her throat. Then her pace increased along with the suction of her mouth. Like a thief that was determined to steal his seed, she master fully used the juices of her mouth, her tongue and her lips to deep throat him to the brink of ecstasy.

Suddenly she stopped, stood up and shed her clothes like some exotic snake shedding its skin.

"Let me fix you something to drink. I got some coke, too. It'll make you feel good, make all your pain go away. Then I can finish freakin' you. You like how I suck dick?" Game licked her lips.

All Rasheed could do was nod his head in submission as his dick stood straight up like a black cobra about to strike. The next few nights he would spend sleepless with Georgia Mae. She did things to his body that he had only imagined.

Fourteen

DieHard Records

The crew waited in the hallway. Mr. Cobin sat perched be-hind his desk as if he had been waiting on them. There were also three other men in the room. Jack only recognized one, David Steel.

The other two men sat to Cobin's right. They watched Jack with such an intense glare that it spooked him. Something definitely wasn't right. It was as if the two men were studying Jack.

Cobin spoke slow and deliberately. "I want you to meet a couple of my close associates, Mr. Springer," he pointed to his right, "is with the FBI agency here in New York, and beside him is Captain Brooks. He's with NYPD."

"Damnit!" Jack cursed under his breath, regretting that he hadn't brought one of his high-powered lawyers to the meeting.

"However, I first want to congratulate you on the success of the album," Cobin said with a fake smile. "The other four acts on the label are also doing well, better than I had ever expected. And the whole New York thing you did with G-Solo's album, brilliant move."

As Cobin talked, Jack made a face that said, "cut the bull-shit." Cobin read Jack's body language and went straight to the point. He exhaled deeply and said, "I'm afraid we're going to have to renegotiate the contract. We've got a major problem. Agent Springer has been investigating DieHard Records for some time now. There appears to be some type of tax violation. Isn't that right, Mr. Springer?"

The agent nodded his head. He was neatly dressed in a gray suit, starched white cotton shirt and matching tie. The man looked to be no older than thirty. He had a bad case of acne on both of his hollow cheeks.

As he cleared his throat, he spoke with polished English. "It appears that one million dollars was used in the production of the album and taxes for this amount were never reported to the IRS. Since your name is on the label as CEO and President of DieHard Records, the government is prepared to hold you accountable. However, this matter can be resolved. In order to avoid having any charges pressed against you, you must with-draw your name from the contract and allow Mr. Cobin to renegotiate."

Jack stood up, stunned beyond belief. There was no better cross than the double cross. They were putting the press game on Jack and it wasn't just that, Jack's lawyers had hidden the million dollars in a mountain of paperwork. The money had come from his pocket to help pay 40 and the rest of the rappers. Jack had a gut feeling that someone had tipped the feds off. He had only told one person.

The agent continued, "Hopefully, we can get this straigh-tened out today, without the government having to freeze all of DieHard's assets. It's also my understanding that you have an athletic shoe contract, and a deal for the movie soundtrack to "Life". Those too will have to be thoroughly investigated."

Jack thought he detected a hint of a smile on the white man's face. He could feel his heart thumping in his chest as he now realized how foolish it was for him to come into this so-called meeting without his lawyers.

Captain Brooks cut in. "I knew your father," he said, unable to mask the venom in his voice as he twisted his thin pale lips like he wanted to spit.

Jack cut his eyes over to G-Solo. Somehow he had distanced himself from Jack as he stood on the carpet chewing on his bottom lip, eyes cast to the floor. That's when Jacknoticed that the door was slightly ajar. The MTV cameramen were filming the meeting.

"Your father, Jack Lemon, Sr., was one of them damn mili-tants. He stirred up trouble for the good coloreds that didn't want to have nothing to do with that black and proud non-sense."

Brooks stopped talking and made a face that indicated his hate. "Now you tryna act just like your father."

"What the hell my father got to do with this?" Jack raised his voice, taking a step forward.

"I was right there when they killed him. Gunned him down like a mad dog," Brooks said with a satisfied grin on his face.

Jack frowned as he looked at him. What Jack didn't know was that Brooks was terrified of him. He was the spitting image of his father, the man whose head he put a bullet in. Now, like some cruel and evil joke straight out of the twilight zone, Jack Senior was back.

Carefully, with a pained expression, Jack looked at each man in the room long and hard. It was then that he noticed that the room was short two chairs, purposely done to make Jack and G-Solo stand. Jack stood up and firmly placed his hands on the desk, knocking over one of Cobin's family portraits. Then he slowly leaned down, inches from Captain Brooks' face. Jack spoke with a menacing scowl, a deep timbre that sent chills through Brooks.

"Keep my ole man's name out 'cha fuckin' mouth. Okay."

It took Brooks a second to gather his thoughts. The resem-blance was so uncanny. Brooks snapped out of whatever trance he was in and sprang to his feet with surprising quickness for a man his size.

"Nigger, don't you ever fucking threaten me!" Brooks shouted. "You'll end up just like your father! I run this city!" Brooks said, pointing a trembling finger in Jack's face.

It took everything in Jack's power to hold his tongue. That old white man had called him a nigger to his face. Jack prayed that the MTV crew was filming Brooks' racist tirade. Jack then moved to the side to give the cameraman a clear view.

With steely calmness, Jack spoke from his heart, a voice that was foreign to him, his father's voice. "Yeah, I guess you would kill me, just like you killed my father, and his father, and his father before that. The cycle just keeps going on and on, until my son finds himself standing in front of you." Jack stopped talking and stood straight up. His voice cracked with emotion. "Shit gonna have to change. Know what I mean? Somebody other than black folks is gonna hafta start dying. The only thing a nigga want is to be respected and treated like a human being. I came in here almost three months ago, signed a contract that was weighted heavily against DieHard, but we succeeded. Y 'all …" Jack bunched his face up with anger.

"Now y'all want to try this guerilla shit."

"Mr. Lemon, all we're trying to do is help you," Cobin said with a nervous twitch in his face. Things had not been going as he had intended. "It's really quite simple, one of my accountants made a clerical error, and obviously you have too with the million dollars used to pay off the artists. I'm giving you a chance to kill two birds with one stone. All we want you to do is simply allow us to restructure the contract. That way you would have assistance out of the looming tax evasion charge and a possible lawsuit." As Cobin talked, Jack noticed his jittery motions as a ball of sweat rolled from his forehead down to his long beak-like nose. He wiped at the sweat with his thumb and continued to talk a mile a minute.

"Surely you can understand my position. Come on, let's see if we can work something out." Cobin smiled like cracked glass. "I need that contract back!" Cobin said, raising his voice.

"How much money you willing to pay to get it back?" Jack asked. He could feel the burning stares of everyone in the room.

"How much money you want, pal?" Cobin responded.

"About sixty-five mil along with the rights to buy out the contract and retain the label's name, and a cancellation of all debts owed to you," Jack said.

Cobin laughed a strained chuckle. Brooks had taken his seat. He mumbled something under his breath.

"That's ridiculous," Cobin retorted, losing his composure.

"Take it or leave it," Jack shot back with a straight face.

"Damnit, don't fuckin' play games with me. My offer is twenty million and you walk away with everything — copyrights, royalties, artists and the label's name." As Cobin spoke Jack shook his head angrily with his jaw clenched tightly.

"Fuck, you think a nigga stupid? Twenty million is nothing compared to the money that you're going to make off of DieHard.

Last year the hip-hop industry made over three billion dol-lars off the artists and the artists received less than one percent. The people that work the hardest get paid the least," Jack vented.

Cobin snarled with disdain as he realized his blunder in making Jack the CEO of DieHard. He had seriously underestimated the Brooklyn thug.

With his lips pressed tightly together, Cobin spoke against his teeth as the right side of his face twitched uncontrollably. "Either you renegotiate the terms of the contract on my terms or I'll have that money tied up in the courts so long you'll grow old and gray before you get it."

"Oh, you gonna up dat money." Jack said. He was losing his temper. "We signed a contract."

"Fuck a contract! The only way you get that money is over my dead body."

Jack fumed with a deadly calm. "Be careful what you ask for."

"Get the hell out! Get out!" Cobin stood, pointing at the door.

The two men stared each other down with deep hatred. Fi-nally Jack said to G-Solo, "Yo, G, let's go." Jack turned and headed for the door.

Cobin shrieked, "Leonard! This is the thanks I get after all I've done for you and your mother?" Cobin voiced a desperate plea.

G-Solo stood in the middle of the floor. The moment lulled as Cobin tugged at G-Solo's conscience. "Don't walk out."

G-Solo exchanged glances with the FBI agent and then looked back and forth between Cobin and Jack. He looked like a frightened child standing in front of an oncoming train. To Jack's horror, G-Solo took a timid step toward Cobin, causing the lawyer, with his pencil thin mustache, to smile. Without G-Solo, one of the originators of the street concept of DieHard, the star, the heart and soul of the label gone, Jack would have nothing. Even the million dollars of his own money that he had invested would be lost.

With pensive brown eyes, G-Solo looked over at Jack and shrugged his shoulders, his way of telling Jack to leave without him. G-Solo was staying with the white man, Mr. Cobin.

Regardless of what Jack said about him, in G-Solo's eyes Cobin had been more than good to him and his family.

Jack made a face like a silent threat as he fixed his hand into a mock gun and aimed it at G-Solo—"POW!"

G-Solo caught on quick. Jack was imitating G-Solo putting a bullet into Prophet. It was Jack's way of reminding him that the gun was still out there.

Jack leaned toward G-Solo and said out the side of his mouth, "Yo, playa, if you wanna chill with the po-po dat's cool. I can make it happen, nigga."

G-Solo's eyebrows shot up in fear as his body did some kind of jerky motion and shifted gears as he walked over to

Jack. Jack exhaled, not realizing that he had been holding his breath.

What the fuck kind of time is G-Solo on? he thought. He had taken the nigga under his wing, showed him how to stack bank, and the nigga just tried some shit like that.

Jack walked to the door as Cobin yelled, irate, "I promise both you niggers, you'll never—"

Jack opened the door wide as Cobin's lawyer grabbed his arm when he looked in horror at the film crew.

"What the fu—" Brooks muttered.

"Hey, you! Come here with that fucking camera!" Cobin yelled.

Jack shoved G-Solo out the door and they all took off for the elevator. The secretary was nowhere in sight. One thing Jack learned from the meeting, G-Solo could not be trusted. The nigga had totally flipped the script. Now with the feds watching, Jack had no choice but to plan his exit out the game before it was too late. Not only that, he was deadly certain about one thing—Cobin was a wrap! Cracka was tr ying to take his grind and because of that, he had to be dealt with ... in the way only Jack could deal.

The next day the media was flooded with the news of Cap-tain Bill Brooks and record executive and mogul Michael Cobin's tirade – blatantly calling the two young black males niggers. Every hour on the hour, Cobin and Brooks' faces were seen on news broadcasts in America and in other parts of the world. The public, along with a few social activists, were asking for an investigation. The broadcast touched the hearts of millions of people, crossing the racial boundary.

One part in particular that was played over and over again across black radio stations and TV was the very heartfelt statement that Jack Lemon made, with what looked like tears in his eyes. I guess you wanna kill me like you killed my father, his father ... until my son finds himself standing in front of you.

Somehow, the entire racist confrontation had sparked a fire of debate across America, especially when it was reported that music mogul executive Michael Cobin was attempting to balk on a contract worth an estimated eighty million dollars. It wasn't long before hip-hop celebrities got involved and eventually ignited a movement that created a chain reaction.

Due to all of the media exposure, the sale of DieHard re-cordings skyrocketed. Thug's Paradise was still number one on the charts. Shoe sales also increased by its largest margin ever due to sales of the DieHard athletic shoe. DieHard and its artists were becoming a household name. Some began to call Jack Lemon a young genius. Not only did he get the New York rappers to come together and put their animosities to the side, but they made music together.

It was decided that all the rappers would come together to do a free summit. It was going to be called the Future of Our Children Summit. It would be a three-day event to debate race relations as they related to hip-hop and rap music, as well as to donate toys and clothes to the children. Homeless children were even being flown in from Africa and other impoverished parts of the world.

Pretty soon, word spread and more artists joined the cause. The children's summit was going to be one of the biggest events since the Million Man March. It was scheduled to be held at Madison Square Garden in New York. East Coast, West Coast and the Midwest all agreed to come together in unity. The Bloods, the Crips, the G.D.s and the Latin Kings. Rappers from everywhere all agreed to be part of one of the most beautiful moments in history.

Meanwhile in Manhattan, the Police Department was be-sieged with angry, picketing protesters who demanded the resignation of Captain Bill Brooks. Finally the Mayor was forced to hold a news conference in which he openly chastised Captain Brooks for using the "N word." He promised the angry crowd that Brooks would be suspended pending an investigation.

On the other side of town in a smoked-filled hotel room, Brooks conspired with Michael Cobin to have Jack Lemon killed and to make it look like a rivalry killing. Brooks knew just how to set him up. However, what Brooks didn't know was that the feds were a lot closer to solving the Death Str uck case than they were letting on. They now had a valuable inside informant named G-Solo. The old chain gang proverb was true, "Too much pressure will burst a pipe."

Fifteen

Lieutenant Brown

Brown had returned to duty from his suspension for striking Captain Brooks. Still, he wasn't back at full capacity. He was reprimanded, taken off the homicide division and given a desk job, where occasionally he was assigned to the field – mostly cases that were hard, if not impossible, to solve. He was also given strict orders to stay away from the Death Struck case.

As of late, the case was starting to grow cold, but not with Brown. It tormented him like a demon, to the point that he sometimes acted possessed. The only good news recently was the Future of Our Children Summit. Jack had quickly become a big name in the city, so much so, that he had started taking security measures to protect his life.

He had good reason to.

Brown shook his head as he smiled to himself thinking about the film that had run on all the major news stations. The spectacle of his nemesis, Captain Brown, and Michael Cobin during a malicious tirade spitting out racist epithets at Jack Lemon and the rapper G-Solo secretly pleased him. Maybe there was a God in heaven. "Vengeance is mine, said the Lord."

Captain Brooks was in so much trouble that there was a public outcry that threatened to become a riot with angry blacks storming the police station daily. The Mayor quickly distanced himself from Brooks like he had the Plague.

Now it was Brooks who was suspended and very likely going to be kicked off the force.

Many thoughts about the case ran through Brown's mind, especially the woman in the blond wig.

"Anthony ... Anthony ... ANTHONY!"

Brown snapped out of his reverie to the sound of his name being called. It was 12:15 on a Friday night. Brown lounged at his crib. He was accompanied by a sexy young redbone with a bangin' body. She was twenty-three years old and fresh out the police academy. Brown had been trying to date her for a minute and with a little persistence, fate finally shined his way.

Keyshia accepted an invitation to see a movie. Tempestuous thunderstorms rained through the night, so they decided to go to his place to chill. Keyshia, with her curvaceous body and coal black, naturally curly hair, sat at the other end of the loveseat with her legs crossed. She had gotten tipsy off two peach wine coolers, but that didn't stop her from working on her third. She could not understand why Brown hadn't made a move on her yet. One of the reasons why she was attracted to him was because he was older, and older men had maturity and experience. But Brown's mind seemed to be elsewhere.

They watched a Dave Chappelle DVD on his 52" plasma screen TV while caustic laughter resonated throughout the room.

As Keyshia giggled and laughed the swells of her large breasts jiggled. Her skirt rose up her thigh with each excited laugh followed by a giddy sigh that ended with a breathy feminine purr. Suddenly, emboldened by the drinks, she eased her body to the end of the couch, causing her skirt to rise even farther up her thigh. She leaned forward, planting a kiss on Brown's cheek.

"Lieutenant, you act like you got something else on your mind. You got any orders you wanna give me?" she drawled, the sound of her voice filled with seduction as her double D breasts pressed against his arm.

Brown could smell the irresistible redolence of her sweet perfume mingled with the peach drink on her breath.

"Naw, I'm alright," he lied as he looked at her, their faces only an eyelash away from each other.

She knew that he was lying, as only a woman would know. They had never had sex, but she wanted to, bad. She had practically waved a white flag telling him to come get the kitty. Keyshia wobbily leaned forward even farther and kissed him gently on his lips. He returned the favor. Soon their savoring turned into lip boxing and exploded into a passionate kiss as her tongue darted into his mouth.

She totally surprised him as her tongue fervidly lashed around inside his mouth with the promise of wild lovemaking. She unbuttoned his fly. He unbuttoned her blouse and reached inside her bra. A tender, supple breast overflowed in his palm. Her body felt like a human inferno. He maneuvered her bra and both breasts freed themselves. Greedily he lowered his head, slobbering and sucking, squeezing her breasts. She moaned a lustful tune as her hands frantically tried to tear away at his stubborn zipper.

He pushed her back on the couch as his sultry tongue, skilled and determined, trailed the erect contours of her nipples, causing a small explosion in her panties. He continued to lower his head, anxiously taking a trek down south to taste her goodies.

She gasped as he eased his hand inside her wet panties. She obliged by lifting her hips up as he took a finger and pulled them down to her ankles.

She kicked her panties off and spread her legs ... wide. He lowered his head and his tongue drove for home, down her midriff, stopping only for a nibble at her belly button. She arched her back at the feel of his hot lava-like saliva, titillating her, invigorating her, causing her to throw one leg over the top of the couch in an effort to get in an "all the pussy you want" pose.

He continued his mission like a prowler. Both of her hands found the nape of his neck and urged him to go to her spot as he licked and kissed, her pubic hairs tickling his nose. He eased one finger inside of her, then two ... three ...

"Ohhh, yesss baby ... yesss!" she exhorted with enticement and wanton lust. He was driving her wild.

She scooted up, pushing his head down. He spread her vagi-na with his forefingers and thumbs as his tongue lapped at her juices.

Then a mechanical voice chimed, "You've got mail."

Brown raised his head. He had been awaiting an email from the Medical Examiner's office.

"I've got to read that."

"Nooo!" Keyshia droned, still grabbing for his head.

A mustache of cum ringed around his mouth. Playfully, he tried to kiss her, but she made a face as she turned her head. The kiss smudged her cheek as her arm flailed, reaching out to grab him as he pulled away.

"Daamn, shiiit!" she cursed as Brown walked over to his computer and sat down.

He logged on to check his e-mail. The first e-mail was from Dr. Wong.

TO: Brownson@aol.com
FROM: DrWong@co.medicalexaminer.ny.us
DATE: September 1, 2005, 12:49 a.m.
SUBJECT: Woman with blond wig

I know that you have been removed from the Death Struck cases. It's no secret, like myself, you too are fascinated with the murders and anxious to see the case solved. The information I am sending you is for your eyes only!!!

I just happened to come into possession of 22 pictures at various angles of the armed female that robbed the jewelry store. As you will see, the pictures have been greatly enhanced due to FBI technology. I am also sending you some enhanced markings of the body of Prophet. If you will pay close attention, the markings look like "C7." A C with a line underneath it and a seven.

After reading the e-mail Brown hit "REPLY" and typed quickly:

You're going too fast. I have not had a chance to review the photos of the female robbery suspect yet.

Dr. Wong responded:

This was your case from the start. I'm just trying to help you. You're a good cop, my friend. I am forwarding you everything they have. I know that you can solve this case. I just wish that I could decipher what the scratches on the dead man's body are trying to say. He's trying to tell us something. What? Bye for now.

Dr. Wong logged off, leaving Brown to stare at his screen.

Brown turned and looked over his shoulder at Keyshia. She had begun to put her bra back on. The comedian Dave Chap-pelle said something that made her laugh out loud, causing her pendulous breasts to sway from side to side.

As instructed, Brown clicked on the attachments that Dr. Wong had sent him. All of the pictures appeared on his screen. His mouth dropped open as he stared at the first picture. With his mouse, he singled the photo out and clicked on it to enlarge it. The woman with the blond wig, sunglasses and baseball cap seemed to come to life. Brown could feel his heartbeat thumping in his chest as he looked at the photos. One particular picture grabbed his attention. It was of the woman crouching down aiming, firing a gun.

What really caught his attention was her face. She had a determined grimace as she let loose a shot. Orange fire flashed from the muzzle of the gun. Brown leaned forward in his seat, not breathing, not blinking, eyes bulging wide. He meticulously went over each picture, each angle. What the FBI lab had done with the photos was nothing short of brilliant.

Again, he went back to the first photo. Using his mouse, he enlarged the photo even more. The woman was crouched down, but barely visible was a tattoo on her breast. A partial shirt collar blocked it, but as Brown strained his eyes he could see it, yellow like some type of fruit design. Maybe a lemon? The tattoo haunted him, causing him to frown.

"Babeee, hurr y up!" Keyshia cajoled with a slight slur.

From the sound of her voice, Brown could tell she was irri-tated. He threw up one finger. "One minute," he said as he continued to frown at the screen. He had seen the tattoo

160

somewhere before, but where? He stared at the screen as if in a trance and then momentarily closed his eyes. The woman appeared larger than life in his mind, like some cinematic fantasy, only it seemed too real. She was the same woman he had been dreaming about.

"How'd you hurt yourself?"

"Running."

"Running from what?"

"You need to be careful. The next time she shoots at you she might not miss."

Brown felt a cold chill. He was seeing the gun aimed at him, orange fire.

"Anthony Brown!" Keyshia called out with so much grit in her voice that it startled him, causing him to turn around. "I just know you didn't call me to your place to play with that damn computer. I can assure you that I've got better things to do with my time than to spend it with someone that I can assume doesn't have a clue what to do with me," Keyshia sassed with her hand placed on her round hip. Her bottom lip was slightly pouted.

"Go fix me another glass of E&J and get comfortable. Get ready to get your boots knocked off." Brown tried to sound hip, but Keyshia made a face at him as she shook her head dismis-sively. "That was old and corny. You need to hurry up," she said as she headed for the kitchen.

Brown's attention went back to his computer. He looked at the next document that Dr. Wong had sent to him. He pulled another picture up. It was the horrifically charred body of Prophet. It was a struggle for Brown not to turn his head away from the screen as he remembered the smell of burnt flesh in the morgue the night Dr. Wong showed him the burned corpse. On the computer screen, Dr. Wong had traced the scratches using some type of white marker, so the marks outlined on Prophet's chest looked like "C7," a C with a line underneath and a seven next to it.

Brown scratched his head as he read the notations Dr. Wong had made next to the markings. It read:

Still can't figure this out

"Neither can I," Brown said to himself as he massaged his temples. He was clueless. Then he accidentally did something with his mouse and the markings turned upside down. It hit him like a ton of bricks – a dead man talking from the grave. Brown looked at the screen and the marking upside down looked like 'JL'.

"Holy shit!" Brown cursed. "The killer's initials are JL."

"I'm back," Keyshia caroled, with fresh drinks in both hands.

"Mr. Man, you need to get your ass over here, right now," she said with steel in her voice like a last warning.

"I'm on my way. Just let me jot these notes down." Brown heard her huff as she sat down on the couch. He reached for his pencil and wrote down what might be the clues that would crack the Death Struck case:

1. Female has bright tattoo on left breast, possible lemon or some kind of fruit.

2. The same woman that picked up money from Damon Dice's mother could possibly be the same woman that robbed the jewelry store and killed two people during the heist.

3. Possibly woman and man working as a team.

4. Scratches on Prophet's chest could be "JL"?

5. Cab driver still not located.

6. Suspected woman walks with a limp and wears a blond wig.

7. Armor piercing bullets known as Cop Killers found at the scene of both killings.

As Brown wrote down his note, Keyshia strolled up behind him. "Look, this is not working for me. I didn't come over here to watch you work," she said, putting on her blouse and giving him a look of disgust.

He stared at her lavender satin Victoria's Secret bra as one of her breasts threatened to fall out as she hurried to leave. Brown stood up opening his arms and walked toward her.

Keyshia's voice was muffled against his chest. "I thought I would enjoy dating an older man. Maybe you could teach me a thing or two ..."

"Shhh," Brown whispered. "You made the right choice, let me show you why."

He stood back and first unbuttoned her blouse and then his shirt. She instantly fell in love with his muscular, hairy chest. Next he stepped out his pants then his boxer shorts.

Keyshia stretched her eyes at his organ as it dangled long. Brown walked up to her, his penis poked upward toward her breasts. Keyshia exhaled deeply into a soft groan. She took his dick and held it firmly in both of her hands.

As she stroked him she said, "God, you're big. I knew it would be the first time I saw you." Her breath was a murmur across his hairy chest.

He unzipped her skirt, allowing it to fall to the floor in a heap. Taking her hand, he pulled her to the carpet.

"W … what are you doing?"

"I'm finishing where I left off. Don't act like you ain't never had a man give you head on a carpeted floor before."

She shrugged, her face indicating she had never done it be-fore.

He gently lay her on the floor and got between her legs. He nibbled on her navel. She giggled. He then took his tongue and drove it all the way downtown to her anus, exploring every crevice and curve, making her body tingle in parts she didn't even know existed. She was suddenly overcome with a sensation she had never felt before in her life.

What is he doing down there? she thought.

Within minutes, he turned her body into a waterfall in his mouth as she came in gushes without end. She moaned and groaned as her toes splayed wide while his fervid tongue molested her body.

Brown closed his eyes and enjoyed himself as he made love to the young woman, the woman that walked with a limp. The woman who would attempt to kill him again … one day soon.

Sixteen

Jack Lemon and the Blood Bath

A few weeks before the summit, a media blitz like never before hit New York City. TV journalists from all over the world were present. It was the first time that all the rappers had come together in unison. Some said it couldn't be done.

Jack sat in the spacious office he had rented in downtown Brooklyn. He was surrounded by a team of prominent enter-tainment attorneys and a civil suit attorney, in addition to two consultants and his PR people. G-Solo's album was already double platinum and was expected to reach eleven million in sales worldwide. Two records were already on the top ten list. Everything was looking lovely.

The murmur of soft voices filled the room. Jack's new secretary entered, causing a few heads to turn. She handed Jack an envelope with a bright gold seal on it.

"S'cuse me a second," Jack said as he looked at the envelope and opened it. It was from 40:

Jack,

So, this is the respect I get? I don't think you have learned to appreciate the value of my work or me as an artist. When we were shorties, I used to look up to you. You had my back then, but now I'm tired of putting cats onto you and you turning around and spitting in my face. I think the latest move you made was a bitch move, something said for pure shock value. Now you're turning against me just like the rest of them fake-ass niggas.

You talk about guns. We got them too and an army of loyal niggas that don't mind bleeding to wet your ass up. I did twelve tracks on G-Solo's album, helped you ink a deal for the soundtrack to the book that they just turned into a movie, Life. As you have failed to recognize, now-a-days I'm a force to be reckoned with. You shall learn.

Do me a favor and stay away from the summit. If you don't, I promise you I'll teach you a lesson about not staying loyal.

Till we meet, pistols poppin'

Fake-ass nigga!

After Jack read the letter he was baffled as to what the hell 40 was talking about. 40 was his man. He was like fam. Jack pushed it out his mind, making a mental note to get back at him. Jack figured, more than likely, somebody had just dropped some salt on him. Jack continued with his meeting, though his mind continued to drift back to 40's letter:

Pistols poppin... fake-ass nigga ...

On the other side of town, 40 was baffled as well. Just yes-terday, he had received a letter signed by Jack. In the letter, Jack was calling him a punk-ass nigga, stating that he was going to check him and that the twelve tracks that 40 had done on the album wasn't shit. Jack and DieHard Records was going to blow up without his help. The letter went on to say that Jack was going to clap 40 if they ever crossed paths.

The ironic thing was that neither one of the men had written the threatening letters. Once again, like the hand that throws the stone and then hides itself, two black men were about to kill each other in a war instigated by the powers that be – the System.

Jack left the meeting in a mental funk. It was like his mind was trying to tell him something, but he wouldn't listen. Jack walked briskly in the parking lot to his big body Benz. For the last few days, Jack had felt the weight of the world on his shoulders. He had a gut feeling that he couldn't describe, but all real hustlers knew when something wasn't quite right. It was just up to him to act on it.

There was a small voice in the back of his head telling him to take the money and get ghost. Jack had been informed by one of his attorneys that Cobin, true to his word, had gone to his own attorneys and filed a lawsuit. The judge had frozen all incoming funds from the sale of DieHard records. Still, the business account had over twenty-six million in it—money that Jack had access to.

Too many people had families to feed. They were relying on his guidance. There was no way he could pull a stunt like that. Jack prided himself on the very concept of Black owned and operated. Besides, Cobin probably wanted him to take that money and run, that way the lawsuit would be settled.

On the highway, Jack drove past plush green scenic pastures while he listened to his all-time favorite classic old school joint by Jay Z, entitled, "Brookyn Go Hard"

He boomed the customized fifteen-thousand-dollar system as he zoomed between lanes headed for a destination to see his lady Gina. He had found a nice spot a long time ago in a rural area just outside of town. Old habits are hard to break, from his hustlin' days to now being legit.

A nigga ain't comfortable if he don't have a honeycomb hi-deout – a stash spot for a nigga to get missin'. Jack had even had a special hidden underground passage added to it just in case he needed to get away from the 'folks'. To some it would have been considered country as hell, but to cats in the game, they knew it as a gangsta's retreat.

Jack still longed for Philly blunts packed with dro and something to sip on but he still wasn't fuckin' with it. Game had schooled him good, but Jack had plans for her slick ass, too. He ruminated as he drove down the highway. If only he would have taken the time to look in his rearview mirror, he would have seen his assassins, sent on a mission to murder him.

Seventeen

Monique Cheeks

Monique arrived back from Brazil and took a cab directly to Rasheed's condo. It was in the wee hours of the morning. It had been two weeks since Rasheed had injured his knee in the basketball game. She found the key under the mat just as he had said in their last conversation.

Well, I guess he ain't that mad at me, she thought to herself.

She opened the door with her arms full of Louis Vuitton luggage and hands full of gifts for her man and her child. Her job as a model had been all that she had expected and more. For one thing, she had no idea just how stressful and tiring the job would be, but it was a lot better than being a stripper and the pay was excellent.

More than ten thousand dollars a day. It was worth it, she thought.

After she placed her luggage on the floor, she swept over the elegance of the décor in Rasheed's newly furnished condo. There was a cozy fireplace, cathedral ceilings, Afrocentric paintings on the walls and plush carpeting so thick that Monique had to remind herself to pick up her feet when she walked. She padded across the living room toward the master bedroom. She thought her nose picked up a faint whiff of something.

Her heart fluttered as she thought about Rasheed being home alone, suffering with a broken leg, and not being able to get home to him in time to be by his side. It deeply disturbed her, but it was her first job assignment and there was no way that she could come home without the risk of ruining her career.

Monique opened the door to their bedroom and a foul odor hit her in the face, a musky odor that no woman could deny – sex. On the other side of the room, music played softly as she adjusted her eyes to the dim lights.

What Monique saw made her knees buckle. Game was straddling Rasheed in bed as she tossed her hair back, riding, galloping like she was on a wild stallion as he palmed her ass, thrusting in her and causing her neck to snap back. Game moaned a love song. Her long blond hair rose and fell.

Monique just stood there frozen as her eyes began to water. It felt like she was melting, losing a vestige of her womanhood, as she watched another woman make love to her man.

"RA-SHEEEED!" she screamed, rising on the balls of her feet, fists clenched tightly.

The thin expensive leather strap on her purse fell off her shoulder. Game looked back at Monique and dove off Rasheed, taking the cover with her, leaving his dick to dangle crookedly like a bent flagpole.

Monique turned on the light. On the nightstand was a plate full of coke and all over the room were empty beer bottles. In the back of Monique's mind she thought about the desperate phone call she had made to Game, asking her to check on her man. Game stared at Monique with the covers pulled up to her chin. The normally talkative Game was quiet.

"I can explain everythang, Mo," Rasheed said, high off coke, geeking with his eyes wide open like a wild man about to have a massive heart attack.

"Explain! Explain what? How my man and my so-called best friend are in my muthfuckin' bed fuckin'!" Monique screamed.

She was livid.

Game propped her feet on the floor as she pushed a ringlet of hair from her face with the back of her hand. She muttered, barely audible, "I'm sorry, Fire—"

"Bitch, I bet you are sorry," Monique screamed. "Sorry enough to want to steal my man! I knew you wanted a black man, but I never thought you would stoop so low as to want mine," Monique said angrily as tears ran down her cheeks.

Game stood and began to put on her jeans. Monique walked over to the dresser, picked up a lamp and hurled it at Rasheed. Barely missing him, it crashed over his head. Game had the nerve to turn and give Monique a defiant look as she leered at her from the corner of her eyes.

"Rasheed! How can you do this to us, to our baby? This bitch, she ... she don't love you, not like I do," Monique cried.

Again, Game muttered, "I'm sorry."

She walked over to the other side of the room, retrieved a credit card from her purse and began to scoop the cocaine off the plate into a plastic bag.

Monique wiped her eyes with the back of her hand. "Junkie bitch, you'd fuck a snake if it was black," Monique hissed.

Rasheed struggled to get his leg on the floor. He grunted in pain as he threw a smoldering look Monique's way. He said to her, "It's all your fault."

"My fault?" Monique retorted, snaking her neck as she pointed a finger at herself.

"When I hurt my leg you could have taken the time from your precious job to come home and be with me as a real wife should."

Monique clenched her teeth as she looked between both of them with pure hatred. It dawned on her, he was jealous of her career. "Nigga, puh-leez, you're just a dumb-muthufacka. A white woman's dream is to have an NBA player. You can have him, you trifling-ass hoe," Monique spat as she narrowed her teary eyes at Game.

Monique mopped at her eyes as she had a second thought.

"Both of y'all got ten minutes to get the fuck out my muthafuckin' house ... or I'm callin' the police."

Rasheed looked at her in amazement. "This ain't yo' shit in here. I paid for it."

"We'll see 'bout that when the police get here then," Moni-que quipped.

They began to argue back and forth as Game walked around the room gathering her things, mostly drug paraphernalia.

Monique thought she saw something that looked like a crack pipe. Monique quickly thought, Fuck that! She had a trick or two for her ass. She knew the white girl knew that Bruce Lee shit with her feet, but Monique was way too deep into her feelings.

"I ain't gonna tell you no muthafuckin' mo', get your shit and go with yo' slut-trash, hoe-ass."

Game momentarily looked at Monique and glared with a facial expression that said "you better watch your mouth."

The two women stared at each other with piercing glares. Monique could see the confidence in Game's face, like 'I just fucked your man, get over it.' Besides, she knew that Monique, being smaller, was no match for her.

"You were the one who told me to check on him because you were too busy with your job, flying around the world," Game said sarcastically. Her statement caught Monique com-pletely off-guard.

This bitch was jealous of me all this time, Monique thought to herself. "I never told you to fuck my man," Monique huffed.

"Well, maybe if you had been giving him what he needed, instead of trying to imitate a model, he would not have had to come to me," Game sassed, heaving her breasts forward.

Monique's mouth dropped wide open with that statement as she watched Game walk over to Rasheed and say, "Give me a call when you get things straightened out around here."

"No, she didn't just try me like that," Monique fumed as she stood rigid, seeing blood.

She stood in front of the bedroom door with no intentions of moving as Game walked toward her to exit the room. With all her might and all the strength she could muster she reached back and hit Game in the face, causing her head to violently hit the door frame. Two more blows and one hard punch had Game on the floor as blood rushed from her nose and the back of her head.

Monique quickly danced out the way and reached into her purse removing the key chain with the knife attached.

"Bitch, so help me God, I'ma cut 'cha if you don't get the fuck out my house … and take that sorry-ass nigga with you!"

"Monique, girl, why did you hit her like that?" Rasheed yelled, eyes wild like he was having a bad coke experience.

He hobbled over and stood between the two women. Game's nose continued to pour blood, staining the white carpet. She was still bent over, semi-conscious. Rasheed caressed her back, then suddenly from somewhere deep in Game's chest a sigh gave birth to a sob that crescendoed into a high pitched wail as she began to cry. She held her hand over her face to stop the bleeding. It only seemed to get worse. Her nose was disfigured.

Monique looked at the two pathetic people who used to be a big part of her life. She had a black woman's scorn written all over her face, lips pressed tightly across her teeth. Her pain was that of a young woman who had been exposed to so much hurt as she looked at Game and Rashed with disdain, her eyes narrowed into tiny slits.

Out of pure malice she kicked Rasheed in his leg, the broken one with the two hundred and eight stitches and all kinds of pins and steel in it. He fell to the floor in excruciating pain as he hold his leg.

"Nah! Nah! muthafucka," she pointed in his face as he lay on the floor in a heap holding his leg. "So help me God, I'ma kick you again if you don't get the fuck out!" Monique threatened.

"Okay, okay," Rasheed said, grimacing in pain as he held his hand out in front of him to ward off her next blow.

As he looked up at her, he was baffled as to where black women store all that pent-up rage.

Monique acted like a deranged maniac as she raced around the house grabbing all of Rasheed's clothes and other personal items, throwing them out into the hallway.

Moments later, after Monique had called a cab, Rasheed hobbled out the door with Game. The pair was a sight to behold. His reconstructed knee would more than likely have to have surgery all over again.

Eighteen

As Jack pulled his car into the circular driveway, he was still bumping the Jay-Z joint. The plush green surroundings were enough to have a serene, relaxing effect on his mind. The five-acre home that he and Gina had rented was situated in an enclave of beautiful trees and brush. There was a fabulous cobblestone driveway lined with bushes and exotic flowers.

As Jack pulled up, he noticed Gina's Jeep parked in the drive. He grabbed his Glock from the seat and looked up to see her smiling at him from the large picture window. Jack exited the car, still looking up at her.

With his Glock in hand, he saw the smile fade on her face, only to be replaced by a frantic look of horror as she pounded the window, gesturing for him to turn around, look behind him. The glass was too thick for Jack to hear what she was saying, but he did catch on to her warning

It was too late!

He spun around with his burner up. The masked gunman stepped out the bushes about ten yards away and fired three shots. The blast lifted Jack off his feet. In the distance he could have sworn he heard Gina scream or perhaps it was an angel, his mother. His whole life flashed before his eyes as he lay on his back helpless, powerless to move. He saw the shadow and heard a car come to a screeching halt. A passenger door opened, a voice yelled, "Make sure he's dead!"

As Jack lay on his back he thought about 40, and he thought about Cobin. He thought about how somebody had caught him slipping.

The gunman walked over to Jack and stood over him and at close range. He fired three more times into his chest, causing his lifeless body to jerk with the impact of each shot.

Afterward, as the gunman ran toward the waiting car to make his getaway, a salvo of shots rang out, KA-BOOOM!KA-BOOOM! KA-BOOOM! KA-BOOOM! Gina was bustin' the big ole .44 out the window, spraying glass everywhere. The big gun nearly knocked her down, but somehow she managed to hit the assassin. The impact of the bullet flipped him, taking a large chunk out of his back. The driver managed to reach out of the car and pull his dying partner inside the vehicle before he sped off.

Gina ran out the house barefoot and crying as Jack lay on the ground. She kneeled beside him, weeping. She cried as she reached down to cradle his body in her arms.

"Help meeee! Somebodypleeeezz, help meeee."

Her sobs racked her body as she swayed from side to side with Jack in her arms. As her tears wet Jack's face, his eyes suddenly fluttered and opened. He was struggling to breathe as he took long, anguishing gulps of air. Gina looked down at him in shock that he was still alive. It was then that she noticed that he was motioning with his hand, trying to tell her

something. Abruptly, she cut short her cries of despair and placed her ear to his mouth.

He muttered, "My … chest …" as he continued to gasp for air, he writhed in her arms in agony.

Gina unbuttoned his shirt. To her utter surprise, Jack was wearing a bullet-proof vest. She had forgotten he told her that he was going to start taking extra security measures. Gina laughed through her tears and began to frantically peck Jack's face with slobbering kisses as she held him in her arms. He winced in pain, struggling to breathe as he tried to push her away with a weary forearm.

"Baby, you're alive … you're alive!" she cried with joy as she held him to her bosom, her body slightly rocking back and forth.

"I'ma call an ambulance."

"No!" Jack muttered and winced in pain as he continued to try to catch his breath. The impact of the bullets had knocked the wind out of him. Next to him, on the ground, was a trail of blood.

Gina saw Jack glance down at it. She read his thoughts.

"I got 'em, baby. I blew his whole fuckin' back out." She smiled, teary-eyed with a sneer, her top lip curled upward.

"You … gotta … take me to Grandma Hattie's … house," Jack managed to say.

Gina nodded her head and attempted to lift him to his feet. Jack howled in pain as he held onto Gina's neck. Excruciating pain ricocheted throughout chest.

After the draft and receiving his signing bonus, Rasheed bought his grandma a house on the east side of Brooklyn. Rasheed and Jack had not spoken to each other since the day Rasheed had called Jack to tell him about the tragedy of his broken leg. Rasheed also told Jack that he and Monique had broken up. At the time Jack didn't think nothing of it. Rasheed and Monique always fought and broke up, but when Rasheed asked to borrow ten grand, a light went off in Jack's head. Because his man had gotten picked so late in the draft, he only signed a one-million-dollar contract which, by NBA standards, really wasn't a lot of money.

Rasheed picked up his phone on the third ring. His voice sounded groggy, weak, like maybe he was high off something. Jack quickly filled Rasheed in on the attempt made on his life. In the back of his mind, as he talked to his old friend, he could tell something was not right. He then heard a voice that he would never forget ... Georgia Mae.

"Yo, son, who is the broad I hear in the background?" Jack raised his voice and felt a sharp pain in his chest as he absent-mindedly rubbed the area that hurt the most.

Silence came from the other end of the phone, then a muf-fled sound, like someone had their hand over the receiver.

"Damn, nigga, who's dat in the background?" Jack inquired again.

"It's Game," Rasheed finally answered.

Silence.

Jack held onto the phone tightly, only his heavy breathing could be heard on the other end. Jack was enraged. "Nigga, what da fuck you got that slut over there for? You got a woman and a child!" Jack exploded.

"You ... you don't understand," Rasheed exclaimed. "Game was here for me when nobody was. Fuck dat bitch Monique! All she cares 'bout is her damn career. She don't love me no mo'."

Jack shook his head as he held the phone. "Listen, B, not the family, yo. Stay sincere to the family. That's all we got as black men, know what I mean? A man's family is his prized possession. Once he gives that up, what's the sense in livin'?" Jack lowered his voice to a gravelly tone. "Dat white bitch ain't no good. Word is bond!"

Jack could hear Rasheed smack his lips over the phone. "You know what? I'm sick of people telling me what's good for me. Since we was shorties your head been fucked up with that racist shit. I think all you niggas be jealous when you see a nigga with a white chick. Jealous because you can't have her."

"What?!"

"Yeah, you know it's the truth. Well, I'ma do me. Game came into my life at a time when I was in a lot of pain. It's just that you got so much hatred for white folks that you think all white folks is bad."

"Nigga, I ain't never said that. What she do to ya, suck yo' dick and blow up in yo' ass? I dogged her ass—"

Click!

Rasheed hung up the phone. Jack was irate. Fuck going to Grandma Hattie's house. He let Gina wrap his chest with a gauze bandage, took a few of her pain killers and suited up for war. Jack was preparing to bring the pain in the worst way. Fuck everything!

Someone had made an attempt on his life ... but they had failed. Jack got on the phone then went to his old hood, re-cruited two of the most grimy niggas he could find, cats that was loyal to the streets. Mayhem and murder was the order of the day. Jack didn't simply want to kill; he wanted to make an example by massacring a bunch of muthafuckas in cold blood—to send a message to the streets. Within four days he and his clique of thugs would go on a killing spree that would equal the number of killings for the rest of the United States that year. He set his sights on the big wigs first, the rich crackas in corporate America.

On a warm Tuesday night, Michael Cobin and his lawyer went out to celebrate. One of his confidants had informed him that Jack Lemon had been taken care of, shot several times in the chest at close range. They went out to one of Cobin's favorite eateries, an Italian restaurant on Arthur Avenue. With Jack gone and G-Solo under his thumb, Cobin and his lawyer made a toast to more money as they sat in the back of the restaurant that had for years refused to serve blacks.

However, it did that day. As his lawyer, David Steel, anxiously looked over some forged documents, Cobin rubbed his hands together with glee. Never again would he make a mistake like that, underestimating one of those young thugs. Making Jack Lemon the CEO and President of DieHard with total control was a very bad business move that could have cost him millions of dollars.

Cobin looked up to the sound of commotion coming from the front of the restaurant. A waitress scurried by, panic-stricken. He thought he heard shrieks of, "They've got guns, run."

Cobin and Steel exchanged glances as they looked up from the booth. Three masked gunmen approached and demanded their money and jewelry. Unafraid, Cobin looked up at them with contempt as he complied with their request by taking off his Rolex watch and giving them his wallet, which contained credit cards and about twelve hundred in cash.

Just some petty-ass thugs, he thought. Give them what they want and they'll go away.

A hoarse voice growled as one of the gunmen leaned over him, "Cracka, I told 'cha to be careful what you ask fo'. You said the only way you would pay me would be over your dead body."

As Jack spoke, Cobin could see the slits of his white eyes as he recognized the voice.

Cobin mumbled his last words, "Jack Lemon?" The first bullet tore through his right eye, then the double barrel let loose, knocking him out of the booth.

With a stricken face, the frightened lawyer looked on in horror. "Please, don't kill me. I got a wife and child."

A salvo of bullets pushed his body to the other side of the booth. Gun smoke smoldered like fog as a river of blood ran. The three armed gunmen calmly walked out of the restaurant, hopped into a waiting black Chevy and sped off.

Each day the reign of violent terror continued to seize the city.

The next day, on September 21, Platinum Records CEO, Richard Wright, sauntered into the barber shop in New York's affluent Sheraton Hotel. He strolled over to chair No. 7, his lucky number. Two seats down from him sat a man who resembled Dick Clark. They exchanged greetings as the barber fitted a white smock around Wright's neck.

Today Wright wanted a special cut, something that would make him look younger. Tonight was the big award show. He was to present the award for best new artist of the year. He couldn't help but smirk as he studied himself in the mirror. He thought about Mariah Carey's tight little ass and felt a slight erection. He sure hoped he would be seated next to her this year.

Just as the barber was covering his face with shaving cream, three masked gunmen strolled in the shop with pistols leveled at his head. They let loose with explosions that sounded like Fourth of July fireworks as they riddled the record executive's body with bullets. The gunmen continued to drill bullets into the body to make a statement. The final blast of the twelve gauge lifted the dying man's body from the seat, causing the footrest to go flying in the air.

Ears ringing to the sound of death. They exited the shop. The Dick Clark look-alike had a heart attack. From his hospital bed he told authorities he saw "NOTHING." Witnesses stated that the gunmen disappeared into the pedestrians on 7th Avenue.

On September 23, in the Mayor's Ballroom, over two hun-dred people, mostly rich record label executives and owners, were in town attending an annual big gala event. It was a festive gathering of who's who in the business. Three men entered. They were sharply dressed in expensive double-breasted black tuxedos and were wearing Presidential masks of the late President Ronald Reagan.

At first, everyone at the gala thought it was part of some type of show, that was until the masked men pulled out sub-machine guns with long clips from underneath their jackets and ordered all the men in the ballroom to line the walls. They were then stripped of their cash and valuables. All seventy-two men were then violently cut down with machine gun fire as wives and girlfriends screamed, affronted by death. Miraculously, thirteen men survived to tell what had happened during the slaughter that rocked the city.

For days the killings continued. Some said it was the mob, since they had their hand in the music industry in a major way. Some said it was the work of hit men, but the streets knew—it was Jack Lemon and his niggas starting to gear up for war. Next, one of 40's people got shot coming out a club, then word quickly spread on the streets that something big was about to go down in terms of a body count. Now it was about to be a real bloodbath, with mothers crying and pallbearers at funerals carrying coffins filled with young black men. Jack Lemon was Death Struck, understanding zero!

Nineteen

Lieutenant Brown

When the killings had first started, the Chief of Police, Brown's boss, had pulled him from his desk job and immediately placed him back on duty to his old job in the homicide division.

Brown was one of the first at the murder scene. The place was a bloody mess. Cops were stepping all over the evidence. There was already a superior officer there in charge. For the first time in Brown's career he saw the law from another side. He knew the only reason why his boss put him back on the job was because some so-called "important white people" had been gunned down.

Brown took one look at the two deceased victims as he lis-tened to the know-it-all white cop declare to the other officers that the motive for the murders was a botched robber y attempt. Brown knew better, but kept his mouth shut. Someone had set it up to look like a robbery attempt.

The music executive had his brains blown out. Brown knew an execution when he saw one. Brown noticed the spent shell casing on the floor and bent down to examine it. It was a KTW.

Brown muttered under his breath, "Cop Killers."

He rose and just walked out the restaurant, leaving all of the noise and the commotion behind him. The woman was on his mind again.

For the next few days the media had a feeding frenzy. There were so many killings of white folks that it practically stretched the entire police force thin. Brown didn't care about the bodies anymore; he was numb. He just wanted to catch the killers ... the woman.

A few days later, the killings were still going strong. Over a hundred Black males had been questioned and the police still had made no arrests, nor did they have any leads. As Brown approached his office, the rookie cop, Keyshia, stood out front in his door way. She pivoted on her toes with pure delight when she saw him walking her way. They both exchanged sly smiles. Brown got the impression that if she had been a kitten she would have rubbed against his leg. She wore her uniform skin tight as her breasts strained against the material.

"I was on my way to target practice and I decided to drop by and check on you to remind you of our date for tonight. I'll cook dinner," she said with an arched eyebrow as if waiting for an answer.

He looked at her breasts, wondering if it was her bra that had her ample breasts so perky or if she was so aroused by seeing him that her nipples became erect. "I'll bring the peach wine coolers," he said with a smirk.

"Oh, you wanna get me drunk so you can seduce me again, huh?" she giggled. They both laughed.

"Uhm, err," Rodriguez cleared his throat to get Brown's at-tention. "Lieutenant, sir, I need to talk to you."

"Yeah, sure," Brown said, turning away from Keyshia with an embarrassed expression on his face.

Keyshia mouthed, "Six o'clock," and walked off.

Both men watched her butt sway from side to side. Rodri-guez glanced at Brown, giving him a knowing look. Rodriguez took a deep breath and tilted his head slightly. "We got a major problem brewing," he said as people passed them in the hall.

Brown nodded toward his door, indicating that they should step inside his office. With the door closed a muffled murmur of noise could still be heard outside.

"It started last night. The hospital is overflowing with gun-shot victims and not just that, one of my best pad snitches is telling me that all throughout Brooklyn boroughs, Vanderveer Projects, Crown Heights, Franklin Avenue, Marcy Projects and Gun Hill Road, they warring big time. Somehow the Latin Kings, the Ñetas, the Bloods, the Folks and the Disciples have gotten involved. It's as far away as Chicago and California. It has something to do with that summit for the kids."

Brown frowned in disbelief. "What do you mean? That can't be. That's the biggest event the city of New York has ever scheduled," he said with a pained expression as he listened quietly as Rodriguez filled him in.

Somehow, mysteriously, from the East Coast to the West Coast, including the Midwest, turmoil was mounting like a dark, violent thunderstorm about to break and New York City was going to be the killing ground. Over the years there had been fisticuffs at the Source Awards and other events, only now, it was decided that different gang leaders would step it up a notch with a real demonstration of a gang war.

The word on the streets was the Madison Square Garden, where the Future of Our Children Summit was going to be held, was going to be turned into the killing ground. 40 and Jack Lemon were at each other's throats talking about serious gun play.

There had already been an exchange of bullets where several people in 40's clique had been shot. Things started to escalate from coast to coast. Rodriguez shook his head somberly after he had finished telling Lieutenant Brown everything he had heard from the streets.

Brown walked to the other side of his desk, sat down, loo-sened his tie and unbuttoned his shirt from the top. Exasperated, he cursed, "Muthafucka!" and slammed his heavy fist down so hard on the desk that it made Rodriguez flinch.

"Why the hell is it that every time we take one big step for-ward, we take two giant steps back?" Brown looked at Rodriguez with smoldering rage. "We got all these celebrities coming to the city, not to mention all the millions of dollars that have been donated for all the homeless Black children and struggling parents. For God's sake, there are going to be children flown in from some of the poorest countries in Africa and other parts of the world and over ten thousand children from just this city alone.

Fuck!" Brown sat back in his seat and sighed, blowing air through his teeth.

He continued with his mind deep in thought. "Certain people are going to get a big kick out of this. This city had a chance to make history, now I might be forced to make hun-dreds of arrests or risk having this thing blow up in our faces," Brown said, interlocking his fingers under his chin.

His mind drifted off to another time, another place, but it was always the same scenario, Black folks trying to overcome insurmountable odds. Just like decades ago, the East Coast and the West Coast had started warring with each other, mysteriously right around the time they were starting to come together in brotherhood. Blacks learned of the deeper lot in the 60s and 70s. The source of the friction turned out to be federal government agents, who intentionally set out to undermine one of the most beautiful Black movements the world had ever seen – The Civil Rights Movement. Spies, bugging and break-ins. All types of tactics were used.

This was at a time when Blacks used to protest and march every time a Black man was killed in cold blood by the police. The youths would smash and loot white owned businesses. Blacks were starting to control their communities, create their own destinies.

There were Black activist groups like the Black Liberation Army, the Black Panthers and more. There were even a few white militant groups that stood up for Blacks.

But eventually, with the influx of illicit drugs flooding into the ghettos, along with the work of the Government, a lot of Black leaders became addicted. It was exactly like the crack cocaine epidemic that seized the ghettos across America in the 80s. The devastation, deaths, and lengthy prison sentences that it caused Black people could only be compared to the Slave trade. It may even have been worse than the terror of slavery.

"I gotta go talk to Jack Lemon," Brown said, rising from his chair.

"Talk to him about what?" Rodriguez asked with a raised brow.

"His father was my best friend back in the day. He was a revolutionary, but it cost him his life. The same thing that they're doing to our youth today, they tried to do back then. It worked.

Jack Lemon is headed for destruction. If a man can't navi-gate his present or his past, then histor y becomes a lie agreed upon by slave masters and their offspring." Brown picked up the phone and made a few calls.

Twenty

Murder Was The Case

Jack arrived at his office with a crew of battle-tested niggas. Cats that sported tattoo tears in place of ghetto fears. They toted big guns and they had all done long stretches in the pen. The kind of niggas that enforced fuck or fight rules on white boys and soft-ass, wanna-be ganstas. Cats whose loyalty was mounted like trophies and medals by tombstones.

The sound of metal armor clinked as they all mobbed into the office, twenty-six deep. Jack didn't believe in bodyguards, but he did believe in the home team. He had made his mind up. If them niggas were talking about letting shit pop off, then so be it.

Someone had already made an attempt to do him in and failed. Jack didn't give a fuck about the Future of Our Children Summit or nothing else. Too many niggas was selling death, talking that killer talk. They had Jack fucked up with somebody else. The rapper Curtis Smith had even sent a threatening letter, talking 'bout if niggas out of Cali saw him at the summit, they was going to take his diamond studded, platinum DieHard chain. Jack had made his mind up to strike first. They was going to bomb on them niggas with serious ammo as soon as they reached their hotels. There was no doubt whatsoever in Jack's mind that he was going to draw first blood – take the crime to them niggas first, Brooklyn style.

G-Solo looked up with trembling fear in his eyes as all the thugs trailed in and lined the wall like mafia hitmen about to bring the pain. Suddenly, he had a severe urge to move his bowels. He had been waiting in Jack's office to talk to him about the death of Cobin.

Jack took in G-Solo's appearance. His eyes were red and swollen, half his hair was braided, the other half nappy, like he had slept on it. His clothes, a DieHard sweat suit, were wrinkled. G-Solo had his mouth open as if searching for the proper speech to plead for his life. He just knew Jack had found out that he was trying to set him up with the feds.

Gina strode in last. As usual, she was dressed to a T. She wore a gangsta Chanel outfit with matching fedora and Isaac Mizrahi shoes with a Hermes bag. Her twenty-thousand-dollar attire was her normal shine. She was a gangsta's girl. Ever since she hit the big lick with the diamonds, Jack kept her laced with the finest of everything. Gina would be the queen bee of the posse of killers on that day … and she would love every minute of it.

They rode in a caravan four cars thick. Jack took one look at G-Solo and thought, coward-ass nigga. I wonder why he so damn scared?

"Word, B, you gonna be a'ight, dis my peeps. They fam, know what I mean," Jack said to G-Solo, assuring his star artist it was all good.

Gina walked with a slight limp to the other side of the room. If G-Solo recognized her without the blond wig and sunglasses from the night of the murder, he made no indication of it. One of Jack's men walked over to the window and peered out. The bulge underneath his coat was

194

visible; the man had a Thomson sub-machine gun strapped to his body. A slight ripple of voices stirred as words were exchanged in hushed tones across the room.

After G-Solo realized that they had not come for him, his mind quickly turned back to mourning the loss of Mr. Cobin. He struggled to talk and his face twisted like a man who was having a seizure. None of the heads in the room were paying attention.

They were too busy planning how to bomb on niggas at the summit that was quickly approaching.

"M … M … Mr. Cobin is dead … that man was good to me and my whole family," G-Solo whined.

His facial expression made Jack want to smack the shit out of him. Exasperated, Jack's nostrils flared as he huffed and blew out air.

"Fuck dat cracka! You all on dat cracka's dick even after I done showed you how he been scheming and frauding a nigga out his chips. He stole a lot of money from DieHard and you, you brain-dead-ass nigga. You need to be happy for him. Crackas always braggin' 'bout goin' ta heaven with its streets paved with gold and milk honey. Well Cobin's bitch ass got a first class ticket to heaven," Jack said, causing Gina to chuckle as she reached into her Hermes bag and took out a Black & Mild cigar and freaked it.

Jack peeked his chrome-plated nine. He was about to say something when the phone rang.

G-Solo picked it up, "Uh … uh … uh … ah, nooo!" he said, alarmed with his eyes stretched wide as he looked at Jack. He put his hand over the receiver. "The police is out in the hall," G-Solo whispered. All the heads in the room were straight buggin' at the announcement of the infamous police. Zippers unzipped, buttons unsnapped, a big commotion started in the room.

The door suddenly swung open and in walked Lieutenant Brown with the secretary clamoring behind him.

"Hey! You just can't walk in here," she complained.

"I just did," he responded over his shoulder, his long trench coat twirling around as he turned around looking at the angry mob of faces that said he was not welcome there. Brown recognized each and every person in the room. He was shocked to find the crème de la crème of New York City's criminal elite all huddled up in the room with haggard, but smug, faces. These were men he knew would, at this very moment, kill him.

Jack walked up to him fuming mad. He tried to abate his anger with a tightly clenched jaw as he said to his secretary, "It's ai'ight, let him stay." The secretary opened her mouth to say something, but decided against it, turned and walked out the door.

Gina eased open her bag and slid her hand inside.

"What's up Stone, Lindsey, Legend? What you fellas up to today?" Brown asked with a nod of his head. The only sounds returned were grunts, along with the shuffling of feet.

"What kinda fuckin' shit is dis?" Stone asked, giving Jack a cold stare.

Jack glowered back at him as a few other heads in the room looked about with panicked expressions. On the other side of the room Gina shuffled her feet uncomfortably with her hand still buried in her bag.

"What the fuck you want, cop?!" Jack barked as he walked up on Brown. Jack winced slightly in pain because his chest still hurt from the attempt made on his life. He cracked his knuckles as he rolled the toothpick in his mouth from one side to the other. The rest of the heads in the room was straight buggin'. Cats in the room had arrest warrants, pending indictments and some mo' shit.

"Listen, man, I know what y'all fitna do. It's not worth it."

"You couldn't know what we about ta do, cop. You just come strollin' up in this piece. You could lose yo' muthafuckin' life," Jack spat with a scowl on his face that said he meant business.

Brown took a tentative step back to regroup his thoughts. Evidently things were a lot more serious than he thought they were.

"Please, just hear me out and I'ma leave," Brown said, ges-turing with both his hands, palms out.

Jack shook his head like "do you believe this shit?"

Stone yelled from the other side of the room, "Let the nigga talk and GO!"

Jack exhaled and made a face. A few of the crew had already started sweating the window, checking the spot below. The room was one big electric volt of tension. Brown knew he ran the risk of getting shot, killed even. He swallowed hard with the facial expression of a man that just wanted to make a solemn plea. "Back in the sixties and seventies we gave birth to one of the most beautiful struggles the world had ever seen. This was during the time brothas just got tired of having dogs sicced on them and their children, simply because someone didn't like the color of their skin. Young people your age, dared to stand up and fight back." As Brown talked his lip trembled with emotion.

"They demanded equality to be treated as equals, like human beings. Y 'all sorta remind me of that time with this thing you're doing with the Future of Our Children Summit."

Impatiently, Jack looked at his watch. "Yo, if you come in here wit' dat Officer Friendly rap, save it."

"Damnit, let me finish!" Brown raised his voice with a frown so intense it disturbed Jack, but forced him to listen.

"Your father was the head of the Black Panther branch right here in Brooklyn. They had a breakfast program every morning. They would feed the hungry black children, white babies too of all ages. Give free medication to the seniors. There'd be a line a block long. The college sistas used to volunteer they time, the brothas too. Each and every one of them children went to school with a full belly. They also built a clinic to administer medical help to the old folks and people of all races.

They did it right on the streets or in the neighbors' houses, young black men and women y'all age." Brown pointed at each person in the room as he bunched his lips tightly together like he was holding back some kind of pain.

His voice tremored when he spoke next. "I don't know … but the white authorities hated your father something bad for what he was doing for the community. Your father knew this. The BLA, Black Liberation Army, the Black Panthers and a host of other organizations were nothing but young people like yourselves, barely in their twenties. They became a threat to the government."

Brown continued, "Huey P. Newton started the Black Panther program out in California and it quickly spread throughout the United States. Here in New York, a brotha by the name of Eldridge Clever was over the Harlem branch. At the time, he and Newton were the best of friends. Soon COINTELPRO started sending threatening letters and phone calls to each man as if the other had done it. Pretty soon, not just Newton and Eldridge, but the entire East and West Coasts were beefing and had started killing each other, and not before long, so many black men were dying that it stirred a national outcry.

"White folks started calling for Black men to stop killing each other, saying that at the rate they were going, it wouldn't be long before they would be on the endangered species list. That was also during the time that tons of heroin was deliberately placed throughout the ghettos." Brown stopped talking and wet his lips and made a face at Jack. "Did you receive a threatening phone call, letter or was an attempt made on your life?"

Jack furrowed his brow and swallowed the dry lump in his throat.

Stone asked with urgency in his voice, "Yo, did 'you?"

Jack cupped his chin, thought for a second, while a few of the disgruntled thugs with hoarse voices seemed to challenge Jack to answer the question.

"Mr. Po-po, why didn't ya join the movement, since it was all that?" Gina chimed in.

Brown looked over at her. Their eyes locked. There was something about Gina's emerald eyes that enchanted Brown, holding him spellbound. It wasn't just that, it was her style and grace. She carried herself with a certain air. She had flawless skin like LisaRaye and a body like Alicia Keys. It took everything in his power to tear his eyes away from her.

With his mouth slightly agape, he watched as she limped to the other side of the room to take a seat.

"My ... my family was doing bad; it was hard times. It was decided that I should join the service. I ended up doing a double tour of duty. When I came home everybody was dead, strung out on drugs, or gone to prison ... just like they are doing all over again to young black men," Brown said, and then refocused his attention on Jack. "The sista Assata Shakur," he looked at Jack, "do you remember when she saved your life?"

Jack didn't answer, but he noticeably flinched with the memory of the beautiful woman with the big afro. Brown continued as he now purposely jogged Jack's memory to a period he thought he had forced out of his mind – the death of his father. "The day that the police ambushed the Panther branch on 63rd Avenue she saved your life by placing you in that metal filing cabinet."

Jack closed his eyes and swallowed hard as he relived the vivid scene all over again. The bullet, the blood, his father sprawled on the floor. "I came here to help you, but you gotta help me."

"Fuck dat! You're on dem crackas' side," an angry voice said.

Brown spun around to face the voice. "Look at y'all! Y'all killin' each other all over again. Young men dying for nuthin'. If old dudes like myself can't save y'all, who the fuck can?" Brown asked, as he walked over to mean faces.

Silence.

"Have I ever busted any of you or taken you to jail? I'm sure I've caught each and every one of you at one time or another with dope or guns, but I always took the stuff from you and let you go. If that's being a bad cop, then so be it. Maybe you would rather have a white cop protecting your communities. If y'all don't care, I won't anymore," he shrugged his shoulders. "The only things I'm concerned about from now on are the Death Struck cases."

He turned back around and faced Gina and Jack. "Before y'all start killin' each other, don't do something y'all will regret. That summit is going to be broadcast all over the world Get on the phone, call 40, call them brothas on the West Coast."

With that said, Brown looked at Gina long and hard. "You never did tell me how you hurt your leg," he said, looking at the tattoo of a lemon with the initials JL on her chest.

Her mouth flew open as she watched him walk out the door. No one seemed to be paying the least bit of attention to him or her, but Gina knew without a shadow of a doubt that she was going to have to kill him.

As soon as Brown walked out the door, everyone started talking at once. Brown had got them all to thinking. Stone stepped up to Jack. He was stocky with wide shoulders and had a perpetual menacing grimace on his face. His naturally gray eyes were known to change colors during his violent mood swings. His neatly cropped wavy hair was trimmed so low you could see his scalp. He had a dirty cinnamon complexion with a thin mustache that connected with his goatee. He stepped to Jack with two pistols in his drawers.

"Yo, son, call them niggas. Find out if they tryna make it happen. I ain't tryna to get caught up in some FBI, secret squirrel bullshit like dem niggas back in the day, know what I mean?"

G-Solo spoke up for the first time. "I got 40's number on speed-dial. I can put him on the speakerphone."

"Hell yeah, let's get dat nigga on the line and see what he has to say," a voice intoned.

They all huddled around the phone like Ali Baba and the Forty Thieves. After a few minutes G-Solo was finally able to get 40 on the phone. The sound of a beat machine blared in the background.

40 put G-Solo on blast. "Is this G-Solo?"

"Yeah, it's me."

"You gonna learn what niggas to fuck with and what niggas not to fuck with. One of my dudes died this morning. One of your niggas burned him coming out the club. Now this shit is personal, so you realize there's gonna be some retribution." 40 was speaking with calm steel in his voice. "Yo, that nigga Jack sellin' me death. Leavin' bitch-ass messages on my phone. Tell yo' man a nigga ain't hard ta find. I ain't new to this. I'm true to this."

In the background a voice could be heard saying, "Da nigga get out the joint, take over that weak-ass label and think he can't be touched." Cats in the room with Jack was looking at each other, some with screw faces like they wanted to get at 40's camp.

Others were thinking maybe what the cop was saying had some truth to it. All were uneasy.

Jack sat on the desk with his forehead knotted in intense concentration as he looked at the small beige speakerphone. He took the toothpick out his mouth. "Word, nigga, I ain't never wrote you no letter. I ain't had a message sent to you. Come on man, you know me better than that," Jack said with his mouth twisted.

Quiet. The beat machine turned off on the other side as hushed voices could be heard in the background of 40's camp.

Jack continued, "Somebody tried to wet a nigga up, caught me slippin'. I took five or six shots to the chest. Luckily a nigga had on a vest." Jack heard a rustle of noise on the other end of the phone. "Yo, B, I got a letter too, signed by you. Talkin' 'bout pistols poppin' when we meet."

"Listen, Jack, I don't write letters. I serve a nigga to his face, know what I mean. If you didn't write no letter, and I damn sure didn't write no letter, then who the fuck did?" 40 asked with grit in his voice.

Jack shook his head and growled, "Dem fuckin' crackas, the feds."

"Word?" 40 asked. Suddenly everyone was talkin'. 40 cut in, "Somebody dumped on my nigga. I'm payin' for funerals on this end."

"Yo, B, I told 'cha somebody tried to do me. I took a lot of slugs to the chest. I'm still havin' trouble walkin'."

"Tell me what the fuck is goin' on," 40 barked, heated.

Jack went on to fill him in as best he could as 40 listened. Jack explained the little he knew about the dynamics of COINTEL-PRO. After Jack had finished talking, the rooms of both camps hummed with a deadly silence. If 40 refused to believe Jack's unbelievable tale of white and black men who worked for the government to cause confusion, then mayhem and murder was 'bout to happen. Nothing short of a war.

40 could be heard puffing on something on the other end of the phone, then he sipped on a drink and smacked his lips. "This rap shit, hip-hop, making too much money. We ain't never had to cross over to them. Corporate America crossed over to us. Jack, my nigga, I feel what you sayin'. When I received that bullshit with your name on it, sellin' me death, I had a gut feelin' somethin' wasn't right. Niggas don't send letters. That shit ain't gangsta." 40 took another long sip of something and belched loudly. I'ma put a joint out tonight on wax. You know hip-hop is the CNN of the streets. Niggas be bangin' my joints all the way in Germany. We only got a few days before the big summit so I'ma put out my first message and let the streets know 'bout this Con–Tel bullshit. We gotta try to squash this shit. You gonna hafta fall all the way back."

"Why is that?" Jack asked with concern in his voice.

"Them niggas, Curtis Smith and the Bloods, tryna get at you too."

"Man, I ain't never did nothing—"

"Son," 40 interrupted, "somebody put out some vicious ru-mors on you threatenin' a nigga if he show up at the Summit. You must ain't had your ear to the ground."

"No, B, when a nigga tried to slump me I made a statement, but I'ma tell you this, and on everything I love, if a nigga do some dumb shit, if one child, one sista gets hurt at the Summit I'ma fuckin' snap!"

"Naw, yo, son, you need to chill. I'ma go on the radio sta-tions and put the word out that ever ything gravy, but it's going to take a miracle for shit not to pop off. A lot of things have already been set in motion. Jack, niggas really tryna send you to the big caddy in the sky."

"Nigga, the feelin' is mutual," Jack responded.

40 laughed loud and throaty. Jack smiled and both camps fed off the jubilant vibe as they erupted in laughter, the kind of laughter that comes like a release of too much built up tension. Afterward, they still made security plans and they all left, except G-Solo. He picked up the phone. It wasn't over yet. It was only the beginning.

Twenty-One

The Summit

The first day of the Future of Our Children Summit was spectacular. It was one of the biggest Black events since the Million Man March. It was so huge that it had completely shut down the entire metropolitan city of New York. All the hotels had been filled days in advance as people from all over the world made the trip to the city. To the unsuspecting, the unknowing, underneath the camaraderie, a war was still brewing.

Outside Madison Square Garden, the streets were cluttered for miles with traffic moving at a snail's pace. Black folks camped out and barbecued in the streets. White folks were pissed. For the festive occasion, dozens of eighteen-wheelers filled with toys and bicycles, which had been bought with one million dollars raised by various rappers, were given away to the children.

That morning, for the first time that Jack could remember, he prayed to a God that he felt hardly ever answered the prayers of black folks. He prayed for the children and the beautiful black women attending the Summit. He prayed because he knew the end was near. It had to be. God's law says so. You live by the sword, you die by the sword, and Jack had killed many men.

A rainbow of brilliant light bulbs burst into a kaleidoscope of colors inside Madison Square Garden. The crowd of black folks was loud enough to raise the roof.

Teenage girls could be heard screaming and yelling their favorite rapper's name, some even cried hysterically as all the rappers and other celebrities sat at various tables with microphones perched in front of them. Even Big Dolla and 40 were sitting across from each other.

Gina nudged Jack to get his attention, but he was too busy doing his own security with his eyes. Curtis Smith and the Bloods sat up front in the audience. They had been making faces at Jack.

On the other side of the audience were the Crips. On one side of the stage were all the old school rappers, and all the new artists who had just come into the game sat to the far right. They joked and played around as video cameras from different countries filmed the occasion.

When the charismatic leader of the Nation of Islam took the podium the noisy crowd quieted to a stir of whispers. He thanked Allah for the occasion. For the next couple of hours, different rappers took turns talking about topics that ranged from teenage pregnancy to drug addiction and Black self-empowerment. It was agreed upon that a lot of the rappers would start to run their own record labels.

The entire time, Jack scanned the audience, looking for any signs of drama. The kids were enjoying themselves, but the ganstas had all eyes on Jack, especially the Bloods.

Again it was the Nation of Islam leader's turn to speak. To everyone's shock, he gave praise to DieHard's CEO and President for his brainchild, the first Future of Our Children Summit, where all the rappers could come together. The entire stadium gave Jack a standing ovation, with Gina applauding the loudest.

He told his mouth not to smile, but his lips would not obey, and instead he grinned. The speaker went on to give one of the best speeches of his life.

"Black people are far from being economically and political-ly, as well as educationally competitive with whites and we are going to have to stop placing the blame on them. It's a damn shame …a damn shame, when two white men alone are worth more than seventy billion dollars. That's more than all the money that the forty million black folks have put together in Ameri-Ka. Weee," he drawled, "built this country!" He shook his fist in the air as he gnawed at the compassion for everyone in the packed stadium.

"We built this countr y with our blood, sweat and tears – our mothers and fathers. Our median income is far less than the Asians, the Hispanics, people who haven't been in this country thirty years. We have been in this country since they brought us here against our will as slaves and we still have nothing. Well, Mr. White Man, we ain't slaves no damn more. That's why we have come here for the Future of Our Children. Fight back, black men!" he yelled and the crowd went wild.

He continued, "And to you gang bangers, don't you fall for the okey-doke. It has come to my attention that each of y'all have received threatening letters and phone calls in the night, saying harm was going to come to you. And now, right now, as I speak y'all can't wait to kill each other – shed some black blood." Jack's jaw went slack.

"This system was meant to make you kill your brother, kill yourself, but not today. Listen to me closely. It was the powers that be that killed Malcolm, that killed Martin, and if you let it, it will kill you, too. To you brothers that received the death threats, the threat came from your government. Please, I implore you, for the babies, there can be no more killings, not today, not ever again."

Curtis Smith was the first to rise to his feet, then about three hundred Bloods rose, then the G.D.s and the Crips, and all the gangs that had come to do bodily harm stood.

Jack rose, too, teary-eyed and tired. A lot of people in high places were disappointed. The Future of Our Children Summit was a big success. The summit closed with a speech to the young black women, and the blatantly disrespectful way that rap music portrayed them – scantily dressed in the videos, humping the camera, and how it made women of color be looked upon and treated with little respect.

Afterward, everyone went to the clubs and had a nice time … everyone except G-Solo.

Twenty-Two

Last Call
Jack Lemon

Jack lay in bed in the wee hours of the morning as Gina lay next to him snoring lightly. They were at the country house that Jack renovated. He had once thought of the place as his honeycomb hideout, but since the last attempt on his life it had proven there was no sense trying to hide out. It didn't really matter now anyway.

Who would have thought a gangsta for life would have come up with such a brilliant idea to bridge the gap of the East Coast, West Coast rivalry all through their love for helping children, as well as encouraging people to become entrepreneurs? All the greedy white record executives had backed up, giving the younger hip-hop heads a chance to make some money. That was Jack's work.

Jack listened to the crickets chirp along with Gina's snoring as the soft wind wailed against the windowpane. Then Jack heard a twig break. He reached for his strap under the pillow and quietly tiptoed out of the bed to look out the window. The cloudless sky was black. Dawn was just starting to peek over the horizon.

They're already outside, Jack thought as his heart pounded so fast in his chest that he had to struggle to breathe. He took deep pulls of air like he was drinking from a straw. For the first time in a long time, Jack Lemon was scared. He saw a shadow in the bushes … then another. His palm with the gun in it started to sweat.

Gina stirred in her sleep and reached out for him. "Boo, why you standing over there?" she asked groggily.

"Uhm … uh … I'm not feeling too good. You gotta get up and get out," Jack said, as he spied out the window again.

"Whaaat?" She frowned at him, still trying to adjust her eyes to the darkness.

"Listen, I left some important papers back at the office. Some of them are papers for the DieHard video game. We're scheduled to have the meeting later on today. I also have papers to put the business in your name, just in case—"

"Just in case of what?" Gina's voice screeched, interrupting him.

Jack didn't answer. She sighed and glanced at the clock on the vanity. It was 6:01 a.m. It was over an hour's drive back to Brooklyn. Gina sniffled and yawned and looked at Jack. Then it dawned on her, she needed to go back to the city anyway. She had some unfinished business with Lieutenant Brown. She was sure it was only a matter of time before he figured her out, if he hadn't already. Gina knew he wanted to sex her. She could tell by the way his hungry eyes roamed the curves of her body. She had a plan to seduce him into vulnerability and then kill him.

She showered and changed clothes. Jack was pacing the room.

"The sooner you get back, the sooner I'll be able to prepare for the meeting." As Jack spoke, Gina realized something was deeply troubling him.

212

It caused her to have a premonition. Gina walked up to Jack as she was about to leave. She hugged him tightly and quickly pulled away.

"Jack, you're trembling." She raised her voice in utter shock.

"What's wrong with you?"

Jack took a timid step back. "Didn't I tell you I was sick? Damn! I'm just not feeling well. Now GO!" Jack demanded, not daring to look at her.

He knew this would be their last time seeing each other. He needed to get her out of the house before them folks came. She turned after failing to read what was really on his mind.

"Gina!" She stopped in her tracks, not bothering to look back.

"I love ya, Ma." His voice had lowered to almost a whisper.

She bit her lip and exhaled deeply, "I love you, too!" Her voice cracked with emotion with her back still to him.

She walked out of the door and out of Jack's life for the last time.

Jack looked out the window and prayed that they would let her go. The morning sun was starting to rise as a large terry-cloth cloud floated over, casting a shadow over the house. Gina walked to her Jeep, chirped the alarm and got in.

With his gun poised in his right hand, Jack checked the landscape as he watched Gina pull out of the driveway. The dense foliage around the house was clustered too thick for Jack to detect any movement.

Suddenly G-Solo's red Lamborghini Murciélago pulled up in the driveway. The sun gleamed off the hood of the car as Jack wondered what the hell he was doing there.

Jack greeted his number-one-selling artist with graciousness.

"My nigga, what brings you all the way out to the boondocks?" Jack asked as they bumped fists and hugged before G-Solo could answer.

As they stood in the doorway, Jack looked behind G-Solo and whispered in a conspiratorial tone, "Did 'ja see anything out there? A nigga feel like Scarface right about now. I can't sleep at night. I could have sworn I seen the po-po in the bushes and some mo' shit," Jack confessed as he shut the door after peering out one last time.

Nervously, G-Solo took the time to assure Jack that there was

nothing out there, saying he had checked thoroughly. Jack somewhat relaxed, maybe his mind was playing tricks on him. They walked into the living room and got comfortable.

G-Solo sat on the couch. "I … I … I need to talk to you, man," G-Solo stammered, moving his hands like he was a bundle of nerves.

"Talk about what?" Jack asked with concern as he stood over G-Solo.

"The gun that you used to kill Prophet with, I need it back," G-Solo said as he fondled his shirt.

Jack looked at him and raised his brow. "You mean the gun that you used," he corrected. G-Solo fidgeted even more. "Chill, son. You came all the way out here to ask me that?" G-Solo nodded. Jack felt a pang of sympathy for him. "Haven't I been like a big brotha to ya?" G-Solo nodded his head and bit down on his bottom lip. "I got your paper straight with the label. You don't have to work another day in yo' life if you don't want to. You can live off your royalty checks, not to mention the shoe deal and the clothing line. Nigga, you still got the number one album in America."

G-Solo grimaced and pulled at his shirt again.

Jack strode over to the window and talked to his reflection. Something suddenly dawned on him. He turned around and looked at G-Solo and asked, "How did 'ja get my address?"

"Uhm … uhm … uhm, I got it from your secretary," G-Solo said.

Jack turned back to the window, and it hit him. He glanced up into the horizon and saw a helicopter hovering in one spot.

Jack turned around to face G-Solo. "None of my friends know where this place is. Only my enemies."

Silence.

G-Solo moved his mouth, but no words came out. Jack con-tinued, "Damn, you came all the way out here to set me up."

G-Solo flinched like he had been slapped. He balled his face up and began to cr y. "You told me they was going to give me the gas chamber. You said the best I could get was one or two life sentences. I was scared Jack... I … I ain't never been in trouble before." G-Solo wept.

Jack walked away from the window just as a Tactical Assault Team truck pulled up into the driveway. Jack touched his temple with two fingers, his mind heavy with thought.

Too much pressure … The finesse game … It is better to be feared than loved.

All the wisdom that he had learned in the joint now seemed to come back and haunt him. Gina's beautiful face flashed before his eyes. Jack glanced out the window and saw the SWAT truck as heavily-armed men scurried out of it.

"They … they told me if I cooperated the most time I would get was twenty years," G-Solo muttered between sobs.

Jack walked away from the window just as a marksman had placed a cross on the back of his head.

"You gotta be the dumbest muthafucka on the planet."

"No … no … Captain Brooks, he came to help me. He helped me make a deal with the feds."

Jack shook his head. "You wearing a wire?" he asked. G-Solo cried harder as he nodded his head and sniffled, "yes." Jack cursed under his breath as G-Solo was now damn near hysterical.

Jack walked over and patted G-Solo on the back with sym-pathy. He felt the wire running the length of his back.

G-Solo only seemed to sob harder. "I'm sorry, Jack. I'm sor-ry."

Jack made a face and hugged him. "Yeah, yeah, everything's gonna be a'ight. I know you couldn't help it. You did what you had to do," Jack said soothingly as G-Solo cried on his chest.

A deep voice that Jack recognized all too well bellowed loudly through a bullhorn, "JACK LEMON, COME OUT

WITH YOUR HANDS UP!" The same voice that had commanded his father to do the same thing.

Closing his eyes, Jack could see his dead father's face. A lone tear glistened in his eye.

"It's over for me, I'm giving up," Jack spoke pensively, for the benefit of the wire. He knew them folks was listening.

For the first time, G-Solo smiled happily through his tears, "Yeah! Yeah! Jack they'll probably work a deal for you, too."

"Yeah." Jack pointed with his chin. Together they slowly walked to the door.

The voice bellowed again, "THIS IS YOUR LAST WARNING! COME OUT WITH YOUR HANDS ABOVE YOUR HEAD!" The voice seemed to taunt Jack, maybe the same way it did his father, and not just that, wasn't Brooks supposed to have been suspended? Fired?

Jack opened the door, the bright sun momentarily blinding him. G-Solo stepped out first, with his hands held in the air. All of a sudden, in one swift motion, Jack grabbed him by the back of his shirt collar. He yanked G-Solo close to him, making a human shield. Jack shoved the muzzle of his nine-millimeter to the back of his head.

Through clenched teeth Jack raved, "Pussy-ass crackas!! I ain't never goin' back to yo' 10 by 12 cage. Keep your fuckin' rats away from me!."

POW!

Jack pulled the trigger, shooting G-Solo in the back of the head. Blood splattered in Jack's face as G-Solo's body slumped to the porch floor. Jack rushed back inside, slamming the door shut.

"Is that gangsta enough for yo' ass?" Jack yelled out loud as a barrage of bullets rained on the house.

Jack raced to the arsenal of heavy assault weapons he had stored in his bedroom closet. It was enough to hold an army of police at bay.

Twenty-Three

Gina Thomas

Gina was about thirty miles up the road, deep in thought, when she looked up into her rearview mirror and saw the flashing blue light. An unmarked police car was right on her bumper.

Furtively, she eased the small two-barrel .357 Derringer out of her purse and placed it underneath the dashboard in a secret compartment. As she pulled her vehicle over to the shoulder of the road, she fought to keep her composure. After she had come to a complete stop, she watched the two burly white cops get out of their car and approach her vehicle with caution. As one officer approached, the other stood to the side.

"Ma'am, could you please get out of your vehicle?" he said with an authoritative tone that hinted at being polite.

"Step out my car? For what? I wasn't speeding or anything,"

Gina said with an attitude as she snaked her neck at the officer.

"Ma'am, your vehicle was observed leaving the residence of a murder suspect," the officer said, stone-faced.

Gina's eyebrows shot up. It felt like her heart had been slammed against her rib cage. She tried to play it off, but failed miserably. "S'pose I don't want to?"

"Then I'm going to have to forcibly remove you from your car and take you down to the station," the officer said, just as an eighteen-wheeler whooshed by, stirring up dirt and debris.

Gina thought about stepping on the gas pedal and hauling ass as she looked up to see the other cop at the passenger door peering inside her car. The moment lingered.

"Am I being arrested?" she asked, feeling her legs shaking on the gas pedal.

"No, we just want to ask you a few questions about your boyfriend, Jack Lemon."

Gina killed the ignition, grabbed her purse and exited her Jeep. The other cop walked up and asked if she'd mind if he searched her vehicle.

"Yeah, I mind," Gina said with contempt, as she arched her brow.

The other officer then said, "Come on and have a seat in the back of the car for a second." Gina sucked her teeth as she followed him.

A lone car passed. Gina squinted against the ardent sun as she turned back to see the other officer who had asked to search her car. He now had her door open. Just as she was about to say something, she heard the sporadic crackling of the police radio.

"All units, all units, be advised, shots fired! I repeat, shots have been fired. Two officers and a civilian are down, critically wounded. Gunman randomly firing shots from powerful assault weapon at officers, possible automatic AK-47. Need assistance from all units in the area."

Gina listened as the policeman hurriedly gave the location. Gina's legs buckled, forcing her to grab hold of the police car for support. She knew the location well.

Jack was having his trial on the street. The two police offic-ers looked at each other in disbelief. The one officer who was about to search Gina's Jeep looked at his partner as they both scrambled to get into his car.

"We already had enough help, with SWAT and the feds to take down an army, Bob. What the hell's going on back there?"

The other officer swung the police door open, nearly hitting Gina. "Young lady, we'll get back to you soon."

As the patrol car made a U-turn in the middle of the road, burning rubber, Gina stood in the dust on the side of the road as her hair fluttered in the wind. It then dawned on her, she would never see Jack again.

"Damnit!" She began to sob as she ran back to her Jeep.

Twenty-Four

Last Stand
Jack Lemon

Nightfall, ten hours later, Jack had the artillery barking like he was in Vietnam. He was putting up a fierce gun battle. Inside the home he had an arsenal of deadly weapons, an AK-47, a Mac-11 and an AR-15 with an infrared scope on it. Outside, Brooks was irate. Not only was he no longer Captain, he had been demoted to Lieutenant all because of a black man.

He had done everything in his power to flush Jack Lemon out of the house, including having the electricity and water turned off. They had fired dozens of canisters of tear gas into the house as well. And yet, like some crazed lunatic, Jack strategically went from window to window, room to room, letting loose rounds of deadly ammunition, making it extremely difficult for the tactical assault unit to storm the house because they couldn't pinpoint his location.

Overhead, the media, along with a police helicopter, ho-vered.

Jack also fired at them, along with virtually everything that moved. The entire footage of the standoff aired on national television as a breaking news report. All the boroughs through-out New York watched and waited. The federal prisoners that were fortunate enough to have CNN, watched the drama unfold. Some of them even claimed to know Jack Lemon personally.

Gina, just like everyone else at the scene, was held behind a police barricade where she was forced to watch and listen to the varying news reports of what was unfolding right in front of her eyes. With her heart broken, she cried frantically. For the first time in her life, there was nothing she could do to help Jack.

Finally, Brooks had enough. Three officers had been shot and, tragically, G-Solo's body still lay slumped on the front porch. Brooks ordered one of his men to bring in an incendiary device. It was a small container that held a lethal flammable combustion material.

Jack continued to shoot bursts of rounds from his AR-15, making the police scatter. Brooks gave the nod as federal agents stood by. Today would be the day he would get his arrest and afterward, the feds would pick up the case in a change of jurisdiction.

At least, that was the plan. It didn't seem to be working. The flammable canister was shot into the house. Instantly, the house burst into flames. Gina watched it all with the rest of the viewers. She wasn't the only one crying now. All the heads who knew and loved Jack watched, hoping that maybe he would come running out of the burning inferno. Then there was an explosion that rocked the ground. As fire licked at the sky, the flames roared.

Piece by piece the house started to collapse. Some would later say that Jack Lemon lived how he died, that he was ruthless to people who betrayed their own people but loving and caring to the needy. With him, his dream for a thug revolution died. By the time the fire department put out the fire, the house was nothing but smoldering ruins. Like the father, the son, too, perished at the hands of Bill Brooks.

Twenty-Five

Days later, police authorities finally discovered what was thought to be Jack's remains, and his skull. Gina was still being harassed by the police, as well as the media. Jack had named her as successor if something happened to him and suddenly she found herself as the new CEO of DieHard Records.

Jack's closed-casket funeral was held on a Monday. Thousands of people attended. Rasheed showed up with Game. They had set a date to get married at the end of the year. Game was pregnant, but it wasn't Rasheed's child. He still walked with the aid of crutches. His basketball career was uncertain.

Monique showed up at the funeral, too. She was still devastated by the loss of Rasheed, but refused to let him know it. Gina didn't have a eulogy or a preacher. She knew how Jack would have felt about that. She simply played his favorite song, a song that he had dedicated to her. Mary J. and Method Man's "You're All I Need."

One Month Later

Gina

As Gina sat outside the precinct in her new Mercedes SLK55 AMG, she waited for Lieutenant Brown to emerge. He agreed to meet her after she had given him a proposition he couldn't refuse.

He informed her that his shift ended at midnight, so there she waited. The night was clear and the dark sky was lit with millions of stars. Gina focused on one star. It was bigger than the rest. She thought about Jack's last words to her, I love ya, Ma,, and a lone tear trickled from her eye, cascading down her cheek.

As she looked at the clock on her dashboard, she had three more minutes. She thought about all she had learned from Jack. She had learned from the best. One minute left. Gina unlocked the briefcase that sat on the passenger side and smiled as she looked at the contents. She closed the lid, leaving it unlocked. She got out of her car and began her countdown.

Three ... two ... one.

Lieutenant Anthony Brown appeared at exactly midnight. He looked around and finally spotted her and began walking toward her eagerly. He loved how she looked leaning against her car. He had been doing nothing but thinking of her. When he was close enough, he noticed that her suit jacket was unbuttoned revealing her supple cleavage, including the tattoo she had on her breast. He was hoping to see, up-close and personal tonight, what the tattoo was.

When he spoke to her, he was immediately drawn into those emerald eyes. As if in a trance, he told her to follow him. She nodded and got into her car.

As Anthony walked to his car, Gina opened her briefcase and retrieved her blond wig. She shook it, placed it on her head, finger combed it and smiled at herself as she began to follow the good lieutenant.

Lieutenant Anthony Brown.

As Anthony drove, he thought of all the things he would do with Gina tonight. It had been a long time coming. He smiled as he looked through his rearview mirror as she followed him. An old school tune by Jodeci played on the radio and his dick hardened as he thought about how well he was going to punish her. The ringing of his cell phone pulled his thoughts away from what would be happening at his loft in a few minutes.

"Hello," he said irritated.

"Hello, Brown. It's Wong. You sitting down?"

"Actually I'm almost home. You got something for me?" He slowed as he made a left turn onto his street.

"I just receive the report from the DNA samples taken at the burned house, supposed to be Jack Lemon's."

"And?" Brown said as he parked his car in his usual parking spot.

Gina found a space two cars down from him. Anthony got out of the car and began to walk toward her car. Just as he neared, Wong continued.

"The skull we found belong to Damon Dice, not Jack Lemon." As he reached out to open Gina's door, Wong said, "It seem like Jack pulled a fast one on you and Brooks. It look like he still alive."

"Jack's alive?" he said as he opened Gina's door.

Jack Lemon

Thousands of miles away on a tropical island, women sashayed by in thongs while two men sat in the sand barefoot. As Jack watched the women, his thoughts drifted back to New York and all that had happened. It turned out several big-name rappers started one of the biggest music companies in the world and Tony, as well as other companies, filed a lawsuit for discrimination claiming their hiring practices didn't hire enough whites. The tables had turned, and that was the first time that had ever happened in history, thanks to Jack.

"Damn yo, you gonna suck up all the weed?" Jack complained in a disgruntled voice.

"Nigga, you said you didn't smoke weed no mo'."

"I said, I had stopped smoking weed 'cause of this white bitch name Game, but it's a whole new day. Now pass the blunt, Pac."

"I see now I'ma hafta hurry up and get yo' ass off this island. Auntie Assatta said you was on some thug revolutionary shit, but damn homie you need to bring your own weed if you a real weed head. Ain't enough room for two weed heads on this little-ass island."

"Don't worry Pac, in the morning I'm leaving on the first boat out, heading to Atlanta, my dude name I.C.

having some drama with some niggaz. We did fed time, I'ma help him handle his business until things cool off in the big apple." Jack said as he sucked on the blunt and coughed.

Tupac shook his head at Jack and reached for the blunt just as three beautiful Cuban chicks sashayed by. They was thick, with ass for days, wearing thong two piece bathing suits. Jack's mind drifted to Gina and he smiled. He knew Gina would always hold it down for him, but Brooks had to be dealt with. When he least expected it, he would experience Jack's wrath, only it would be worse than anyone could imagine.

Taking a deep pull off of the blunt now, Jack held the smoke in his lungs and didn't cough. He passed it back to Pac as he got up, ran to the ocean and dived in, catching a big wave. As the wave accepted him, his thoughts drifted back to Brooks.

It ain't ova, he thought. It ain't ova.

Pac smiled, "Thug revolutionary, huh? What's the world coming to?"

A Gangsta's Bitch 2

Made in the USA
Lexington, KY
11 October 2014